Gather Gold
and other stories

Barrie Llewelyn

OPENING CHAPTER

First Printing, 2015

ISBN 10: 1-904958-60-5

ISBN 13: 978-1-904958-60-4

published by

*Opening Chapter
Cardiff, Wales*

www.openingchapter.com

To Ed Volk
1925 - 1996

I have no doubt at all the Devil grins,
As seas of ink I spatter.
Ye gods, forgive my "literary" sins --
The other kind don't matter.
-Robert Service

Contents

Gather Gold

Young man, gather gold and gear
- Robert Service

Get up, get dressed, we're going soon, not much time, make sure you go to the bathroom.

The girl hated the swap meets. She felt like she was being raised from the dead. It was always too early, too dark. It was cold. But she had to go. They all had to go. The girl and her brother were too young to stay in the apartment alone and her mother wouldn't ask anyone for help looking after the kids. Her mother wouldn't think of staying behind herself, missing the day. She loved it – out in the sun and the dust, selling off her wedding presents, selling her clothes, selling old sheets – anything she could find. She loved getting browner each weekend in the sun, wearing a big hat, taking people's money for junk she found on the tops of her cupboards. The girl was terrified someone from school might see her or recognise her mother and father.

Out of pyjamas, into yesterday's clothes, no time for breakfast, we'll eat something later. Quick, brush your teeth.

Saturday or Sunday or both, depending on how much they had to sell, depending on how much more they needed to be able to pay the rent on the new apartment. Last year her dad lost his job and then the house had to be sold to pay all the debts: credit card, car loan. The girl heard them talking about this late at night – not talking – disagreeing, arguing, fighting. It was hard not to hear them, the apartment was so small. It was hard for the whole apartment building not to hear them once they really got going. The girl tried not to think about the people next door and what they thought. But that was hard too, when she passed anyone on the outside landing she turned her head away so she could not see how they looked at her.

This was his job now, buying and selling. It was only nickels and dimes and sometimes it came in slowly. Long days in the sun and wind and dust and not many lookers putting their hands in their pockets to become buyers. Still most months, most of the time, the girl overheard that there was enough to pay the rent and she could tell when the refrigerator was full. That was enough to hold everything together. That was enough to keep her mother from shouting at her father. That would be enough as long as she could keep her brother from mentioning the shoes he wanted like all the other boys. They were called Wallabies and girls wore them too, but they both needed to remember not to ask for anything.

So she hated it, but she had to go along with it all; the vinyl seats in the car were cold. There was hardly any room, the old station wagon so packed with things: old china cups, silverware, some of her father's books and records. And other stuff, merchandise he picked up during the week as he travelled through the seedier parts of the city visiting close-out sales, factory clearances, end of the lines.

Saturdays and maybe also Sundays. They drove through the dark streets, moonless mornings, everyone else in the world asleep. David Cassidy would definitely still be sleeping somewhere in the Hollywood Hills. Got to get there. Get a good pitch. Got to be early. East on the 405 (Hollywood Hills and David were in the other direction) and out to the 5. Sylmar, Newhall, Saugus. The girl tries not to remember, but when she does it's Saugus race track she sees. Dusty side of a mountain is how she describes it. There was a train that went by high above weaving through brown crevices every few hours. She knew she had to hear four trains go by before they could go home.

When they got there, it was just about dawn, but you couldn't go right in. Had to stay in the car and wait your turn. Pay your fee and get allocated a space. A corner was best to hope for or anywhere near a taco stand or the Slush Puppies was good. Her father knew after the second or third time that it was best not to ask for a good spot 'cause you'd only be given a bad one, somewhere around the back stretch, somewhere only the die-hard bargain hunters ever made it to. There was a snake lady and the girl didn't care where they were as long as they were not near those snakes wriggling around her neck reaching out to tourists who passed by her stall. God knows what she was selling. The girl didn't know – couldn't see past the king cobras, vipers and pythons, fat and lazy wrapped around the fat and lazy snake lady. The other place the girl really didn't want to be was next to anyone selling eight tracks; she didn't want to hear music all day long unless it was the music she liked. It never was.

Good kids, good kids. Her father and mother would compliment them when they helped to unload the car. Set up the card tables. Set out the stuff.

This week he had bought hair clips and hand cream, plastic earrings and a pile of cheap belts that looked like they came off cheap dresses. The dresses were probably sold to someone else so that they could take them to another swap meet, Torrance or La Mirada – those were held at drive-in movie theatres. Butter and popcorn and the smell of half-sex from the night before hung over the huge swap meets the next day. Her father was terrible at buying, wouldn't think to get the dresses to go with the belts and anyway he'd have to buy the hangers then too and racks to hang them on. She knew that he always paid too much for everything; could just imagine how they took advantage of him.

Good kids. Go for a walk, buy yourself some churros for breakfast. Donuts, black coffee or, sure if you want to, have a chilli dog, it's never too early.

But the girl didn't want breakfast. She wanted to stay in the car. Now that the car was empty, she could lie across the backseat, cover herself with a white sheet Dad had put in at the last minute in case the earrings had to be protected later from wind or dust. She could read this week's Tigerbeat. Look at pictures of David Cassidy. Her mother passing the window would say, stop looking at that girl; oh it's a boy. The girl couldn't stand it. Her mother made the same stupid comment every weekend.

And now her father had started his day.

Lice Cream, he was almost singing out, Get your lice cream here.

His Shoes

There were shoes by the back door when I came in with the shopping. Big as boats, shaped like black and yellow bananas. Automatically, I bent over to put them away. There's an Ikea trunk for shoes beneath the stairs, for our shoes: Charlotte's school shoes; her flip-flops and trainers; my slip-ons and work-shoes and wellies for the garden. I was going to pick up these rogue foreigners left carelessly so that someone might trip over them and put them with the others. Then I stopped. These were aliens, not mine to touch or move. It's been a long time since there were man things in this house. I left them where they were. But then, at the last minute turned them so that they were on their way out, ready to leave.

I turned away too and shouted towards the living room, 'I'm back,' and as I made my way to the kitchen, I thought again about yesterday and the day before and the weeks before that when we were still on C1. So many days and nights and every twenty-four hours another dose of *the beast*. The doctors called it ALG and tried to explain what it was and how it would help us but they glossed over what it would do to Charlotte every time it was fed into her through her Hickman. *We have to make you ill, to make you better.* How many times did I hear that apology and watch

Charlotte nod her acceptance through rigours and cold sweats and rash? We dealt with it in the way we've always dealt with everything: as they wheeled the metal pole in and connected the IV to it and to her, I only had to look at Charlotte and we'd mouth the word *beast* to each other at the same time. We'd giggle and try to hold that moment as long as we could, tried not to think of how long it would be this time before the side effects – which had no other side but nasty – began.

'I'm back,' I said, again as I walked through to the living room. 'And I've thought if I use Milton to sterilise the lettuce you can have your Caesar salad, I even got you a tin of anchovies – I thought we could take a walk to the shop and get a film out for late...'

The room was empty. I'd left her propped on pillows and surrounded by juice and magazines only half an hour before.

'Hey. I'm back,' I called up the stairs.

'Great. Be down now. Hope you've got food,' Charlotte called from her room.

A minute or two later, she was down the stairs and in the kitchen, the boy was just behind her. The owner of the banana boat trainers. Both of them were going through my Tesco bags.

'Mum, James wants to eat with us, okay?'

'Sure,' I said. 'Hi James, have we met?'

Charlotte giggled and rolled her eyes in exasperation with me. 'Every day in hospital, Mum, James was there.'

I hadn't noticed.

Charlotte's room in the bone marrow transplant unit was purple. Late in the mornings Penny came in to clean the purple room. She had a special mop in a bucket marked 'purple' and with it she moved bits of dirt and hair and sometimes dried blood from place to place. She mopped last, moving herself out of the room, telling us stories about her grand-daughter: *about your age and just as pretty, duck.* Penny was working to pay for her granddaughter's tuition to a boarding school for dancers in Leeds or Loughborough. I could never remember which and didn't like to keep asking. Before she mopped, she'd shuffle the get well cards along the windowsill from place to place so that she could wipe over the surface, commenting all the time on the amount of cards there were and the gifts and all the visitors in and out. *How popular you are, duck.* And Charlotte, no doubt about it, glowed at the attention of this quick little woman, while I sat in my corner chair, lifting my legs up for the mop to slide under. And every time it did, my heart filled with the endlessness of time in that purple room.

There aren't visiting hours in the unit. People have to scrub up and put on a gown, but as long as you aren't actually recovering from a transplant, anyone can wander in to see you any time of day. I scrubbed and gowned but of course I wasn't a visitor, I was there to be with Charlotte: to get her food if she was hungry, to stand outside the cubicle while she showered, to dry her hair, paint her nails, wheel her to x-ray, watch for signs of distress when they attached her to the beast. Run out into the corridor to get help.

I spent the nights on that cold leather chair in the corner of the room under the lamp and the call button. The chair was ripped and grubby with dirt in corners, which was a little incongruous with the sterile gown I was required to keep on while I tried to sleep. A kind nurse gave me a blanket and I put it over that chair rather than myself. Still I couldn't help thinking of those other mothers that had sat there before me just as terrified at two, three, four o'clock in the morning listening not to hospital noises – nurses' tea-cups or the temperature and blood pressure trolley making its rounds – but to the evenness of their child's sleeping breath.

Some nights when she asked me to and when I wouldn't be in the way of her tubes, in and out, I climbed into the bed and stayed till the hospital radio played Dancing Queen at six am to wake everyone up. Those were the best times, when I could hold my beautiful girl, touch her silky hair. Then it was like it had always been, just her and me; no one to interrupt while I looked after her.

In the morning, evening and the middle of the day there were visitors: boys and girls Charlotte knew from school, from various part-time jobs, from nights out. I recognised some of her oldest friends, of course, but I was surprised at how so many youngsters who I didn't know came to see her. I could see Charlotte change when her friends were there. Her colour came back; it was good to hear her laugh. The purple room became a common room in school or a café in the centre of Cardiff and as the room became busier the nurses lingered after their checks, drawn in by the sound of teenagers.

After a while I'd leave them. The coffee shop was also the staff canteen and there were two prices for everything. I drank tea at the higher price and looked straight at the overhead TV. It was usually Wimbledon or highlights from Wimbledon, but it might have been an earthquake killing off the population of Mid Wales and I wouldn't have noticed. I never saw any of it. I was just waiting a reasonable time until I could go back to her. Visitors are a good thing, but they shouldn't stay too long. Charlotte was undergoing treatment, she needed to rest. I needed to make sure Charlotte got some rest.

I should have noticed James. The day after that first supper, she told me about him. He'd visited her every day in hospital, most days twice. How had I missed him? Just before she became ill, he began to drive her home from school. Why hadn't I known about it? He lived nearby she said. She'd known him for a long time, as you know local boys, faces in school. They were just friends, she said.

Just friends. That was supposed to make me feel better about the time he spent with her upstairs in her room. I knew they were lying in her bed together. Most nights he didn't leave until very late, well after Charlotte had fallen asleep. I tried to get used to the bed thing, after all Charlotte was supposed to be resting between daily visits to the out-patient unit for her continuing treatment. I told myself that if they were just friends, this was okay. Still, after a week or so, I couldn't help but mention it.

'We're only watching TV or listening to music,' Charlotte said in a way that told me there was no point saying anything else about it.

I couldn't help but hear her laughter and his rolling voice, the way he was in the house. The way he came in and threw off his shoes, stretched himself out on the settee for a few minutes, even making small talk with me, before they went upstairs. The way he made regular trips to the kitchen to check out the contents of the fridge, make sandwiches. The way he fed her and brought her things. Like my time in that purple room – very soon James was no longer a visitor.

Still, the days with her were mine. James had to go to school and we had our trips to the day unit together. It was a place for the shuffling elderly, for chemo infiltrations and blood transfusions. For Charlotte, it was a place of waiting and being restless, of realising how an illness can shrink your world to the next pill, the next temperature check, the next needle, scan, blood count. I tried to make it better. I bought *Heat* and *Hello* and on good days we studied those magazines and commented on what Victoria Beckham was wearing or why anyone would want to take so many pictures of her. On those days, I could make her laugh in the way we had together, making faces at one of the bossy nurses or talking to her in a silly whisper trying not to be heard, trying to keep everything between us.

There were other times though. And I couldn't help but notice that as the weeks wore on they became more frequent. Charlotte would be uncommunicative; she'd walk into the unit with her earphones on, the volume of her iPod all the way up. She'd pretend not to hear anything the receptionist, or the nurses, or I said to her. She'd pull faces and turn away if another patient acknowledged her with a smile or tried to speak, leaving me to make polite conversations I wasn't in the mood for either. And then when the frustration finally boiled up, it was me that she'd turn on. It was sudden.

'You don't have to be here, you could go back to work, you can go shopping. I have to be here but you don't,' she said one day, the poison from the beast in her voice.

'Charlotte, sweetheart. I don't want to be anywhere else. I want to be with you.'

'I don't need you with me. I know the routine.'

'Don't be like this with me,' I pleaded as quietly as I could. There were other patients close by. There were nurses, social workers, a receptionist. It was afternoon; everyone seemed paralysed around us, connected to a machine. Everyone wanted something interesting to happen. I didn't want us to provide the day's entertainment and I didn't want anyone else to know that Charlotte wasn't just a sweet, sick teenager and I, her ever-doting mother. I didn't want to admit what the drugs were doing to her; what being ill was doing to her. And even more than that, I knew that some of this was about James. She would much rather he was there than me. That was the thought that brought the tears to my eyes. It was the worst thing I could do. She saw the tears and I have never seen her harden so.

'It's not your disease. Why are you crying?'

She said it out loud and clearly. I felt the pores open on my back and under my arms. I felt my healthy blood pound through my body, like it's supposed to. I should have been more the mother. I should not have fled from the day unit. I should have smiled and laughed it off, brought out some Haribo candy, produced a new magazine for us to laugh over. I should have done all those things because an hour later, I had to return and face everything I had not done. Quietly admit to everything I was incapable of being for her. I had to act like everything was normal when my daughter looked through me and then ignored me all the way home.

His shoes are by the back door. Charlotte and James are in the living room watching the Simpsons. I can hear her low conforming laughter – even I remember how you change things about yourself when you are falling in love.

I've been shopping. I've brought them food. Coke and crisps and our dinner. James doesn't like fish or carrots. So maybe, by not having those things on the menu, I can tempt him to stay. Sometimes he goes home and eats with his parents, but he always comes back half an hour later and anyway I need him here more than they need him at home.

I can't help going into the room to see them. I feel her head for temperature, and though she hasn't spoken to me for most of the day, because he is here, she lets me touch her.

13

'There's pizza for dinner,' I say and they both nod and Charlotte smiles at me like she always has.

Before I do anything else – water the garden, pay bills, put the pizzas in the oven, I need to get his shoes out of the way. He's always leaving them where someone could trip over them.

It's late – past midnight and there is no more noise coming from her room. No music or the muffled sounds of their talk and their laughter. I think they have fallen asleep. I wonder vaguely if James has an overnight bag or a toothbrush and then I think maybe I have dozed off and he has gone home. When I think this, I feel my heart stop.

But downstairs, his shoes are in the place where I left them. I pick them up and hold them for a while. They're so big – and yet how big can they really be? I think maybe I should clean them, as far as I know he wears them every day; they deserve to be cared for. In the kitchen I lie them on paper towels and spread the laces out of the way. With Fairy on a J-cloth, I begin to wipe them down, working from back to front. The leather is hardly cracked; I think of how James is gentle, easy on his things. With an old toothbrush, I clean the grooves on the soles. They are surprisingly clean anyway. James is careful where he steps, I think. I start to cry.

I hold his shoes close to my dressing gown and take them into the living room. I open the curtains a bit and see where they have left empty Coke cans and half a bowl of smelly crisps on the coffee table. Preferring the dark, I close the curtains again and sit

14

where they sat earlier, before they'd gone to bed. I begin to rock.

Back and forth, I hold his shoes and rock. I must have stopped crying because now I am humming a love song and floating. Back and forth with his shoes, I am somewhere else.

After a while, in the kitchen, I stuff his shoes with more kitchen roll. It will help them keep their shape and I tie the laces. It takes me four attempts, but finally the bows are equal to each other and perfect.

And then I put them away for the rest of the night. Not in our trunk, but near it. Very close.

Shopping

*H*e's skinny. Not just slim. The back of his arm – when I touched him gently just now to tell him that I wanted to stop and look at the wild California poppies for a moment was twig-like, even through his sweatshirt. My husband could break him – would break him if he knew the things we have been saying to each other.

The first time one of us really touched the other, it was me. No surprise there. It's almost compulsive for me to feel the things I am focused on – like the flower that I bent over a moment later, just needed right then to trace its papery texture. This is the way I will remember it later, the feel of the poppy, the first touch of his arm.

He hasn't come that close to me yet. He got out of his car – a boring white sedan. And clean, I knew it would be clean – and I got out of mine, which looks and smells like a rented vehicle and I thought for sure we would hug like old friends; in my imaginings we always hugged when we finally met. But here was the moment and we both stood where we were – maybe three feet from each other and stared while our mouths moved with words, pleasantries, excuses. Sorry I'm a little late, you look just like... Of course there have been pictures, but I never thought he would be so thin.

16

I kept my sunglasses on purposely. I always look people straight in the eyes and I assume everyone else does the same. His eyes, with no sunglasses, didn't give anything away about his first impression of me. They didn't look as deep and sexy as they do in all those photos he forwarded. So here we are finally and we're both being so polite. And cautious. You'd never know that we've been making love for months.

When I realised that I had fallen in love with M, I began to take the car to a lot of supermarkets. Shopping for food was the one thing I could do on my own. Neither of my girls nor my husband were at all interested in groceries. So I visited Tesco, Sainsbury's, and Waitrose often. As soon as I got in the car I'd stick some pop music on the cd player and sing along to the sentiment of impossible love. That was good enough, but even better was wandering through the aisles of those huge 24 hour superstores and talking to my lovely M. I could resume all the conversations we'd started but never seemed to be able to finish. I could talk to him as if he was here in the same country as me. As if I actually knew his voice. Forty years old, though I'm often told not bad for it, and there I was wandering around talking to myself. Sometimes I only managed to buy a quiche.

The last time I'd fallen in love, I was twenty and it was okay – even encouraged. And it has been all right, really: the girls, a lovely home, a comfortable life. But now twenty years later, I was a wandering nympho in a supermarket.

That's the other thing, when you fall in love when

17

you're only twenty though the sex may be wonderful, you think of love as if it's something that elevates itself beyond the physical. But now the love I felt for M was more about being randy beyond words than it was about anything that I believed would be lasting or soulful.

That may not be right. Certainly when I was driving to Sainsbury's or Tesco (never Marks and Spencer, because the girls would have wanted to join me to look for bras and jumpers), I believed that M had got under my skin and tapped so many familiar buttons that I thought he was my soul mate – and though our love was impossible, it was also destined to be. This is what was going on with me: I was thinking in clichés and song-lyrics; logging onto the Internet at 5 every morning and shopping.

At first our conversations were well behaved, but I knew right away that we shared the same language and humour. What was better was that our sense of humour was wordy and intelligent and it suited the medium. And I could talk to him. I told him my secrets.

We were so good at talking for nearly a year that it never occurred to me that I hadn't heard his voice. Our friendship existed despite time zones. I am an insomniac and he is a bit of night owl. At my best in the early hours of my morning; he was at his best in the late hours of his night. Our early conversations were also helped by the fact that we had known each other once – a long time ago. Okay, he may have been just a face in a classroom and I have to admit, I don't remember that much about the little boy that turned into M. Only that he had one of those names that you couldn't say the first name without saying the last as well, like Charlie Brown. You would never just say Charlie, would you? And he had kind of memorable eyebrows, but other than that he was forgettable; someone I never thought of once I left the west coast almost thirty years ago when my British mother said to my American father, I have had enough, we either live in England or our marriage is over. Eventually their marriage went the same way that mine is about to go, so the big move (as we referred to it) didn't work.

I never wondered too much about the way M found me. It's quite common these days to search out long lost school friends and engage them in polite conversations. And I guess I was a little interested in what I had left behind. American lives are always portrayed to be so much better than our British ones. What I should have wondered more about in those first few months is why he looked for me or maybe what he was looking for at all.

Whose idea was it to meet near the old school and walk the old route? It must have come about from some long ago conversation. I must have told him that I always wanted to go back and see if the old place was still as I remembered it and if I could retrace my steps. He can come here anytime; he still lives just a short drive a way. But for me, it's different – I have to rely on my memory of places and of the people that I once knew. Can't just get in the car and go visit.

He is absorbed as we come to the front gates. Quiet.

While we have been walking here, he asked me how my flight was.

'It was quick and it was long,' I answered. Immediately I wanted the sidewalk to open at its next join so that I could fall into it and disappear. Articulate woman. It was quick and it was long? Where did that come from?

He giggled. I knew he would be someone who giggled and I joined him but after that there didn't seem anything else to say. Not an uncomfortable silence but a quietness between us as if we had not just met, as if we have already done the small talk – which of course we have. And after that first look, he hasn't looked at me again. I am wearing the tight black cropped trousers and a clingy black sweater. He can see the shape of me; I've done it on purpose, but I can't tell if he has even noticed or what he thinks. Not like those times that he has taken off my clothes, and slowly kissed my shoulders, my neck, my fingers, my breasts, my stomach telling me all the while that he loves what he sees. That I am beautiful.

No one I know ever talks about cyber love. Even telephone sex, which I confess I had heard of, was not a common occurrence in my circle of acquaintances. Though now when I throw the words 'internet relationship' into a conversation (just to see the reaction) it turns out, it's common as muck. Everyone knows someone who is doing it or has done it. No one, you understand, admits to having done it themselves. In fact to go backwards a little, that is exactly how I throw it into conversations: I talk about the sister of a good friend of mine who is having an 'internet relationship' with a man who lives in Tasmania. And then what I say (in a low shocked whisper) is: and I am told they are doing it.

The school gate is open. It's a Saturday morning and the gate is wide open, almost inviting us to enter. I have often been the more daring one of us and now he follows me through. We're in. But I have no idea where we are. I'm already lost, I tell him.

'Let's go this way, I think the kindergarten is this way,' he says. His voice I realise is thin too and an octave higher than my husband's. Not unpleasant, but not that attractive either. Maybe that is why he's quiet, maybe he's conscious of his voice. But now he's not quiet anymore.

'Do you remember that this is the office,' he tells me as we pass one of the doorways, ' I once got hauled in here for hitting a teacher.'

'You did what? You were a good boy, I think.' I wonder how my voice sounds to him. I think it's lower than his, and I wonder what he makes of my weird accent.

'You won't remember this, you'd left by then, but the sixth grade teacher held the back of my neck a little too tight and I didn't like it, I reacted and hit her. Sat the rest of the day with the Principal.'

'What was her name again?'

'Mrs McIntyre.'

'God, you remember everything, don't you?'

He giggles again, 'I have a good memory for some things,' he says.

21

But we didn't do it for a long time. After a while it became pretty obvious that we liked each other. Little references between us began to develop. We had pet names for each other. We talked less about my husband and his wife – noticeably less. The messages that we sent to each other in between our long chats got more and more common. Sometimes they were only one or two words; reminders that though we were getting along with our separate lives, we were also very much thinking of each other. He, being far more up to date with technology than I, sent me lots of pictures. I saw my old school acquaintance not much changed: just taller, older, obviously much more a man than any remembrance I had of the boy who had to be called by those two names. Still there was something in his face (besides those eyebrows) that I recognised.

One thing I have learned from this is that for men there has to be something visual as well. Chatting, talking, flirting, words were just not enough for him as they were for me and it didn't really start between us until someone I work with forwarded me a picture of us at a dinner, it was a pretty good likeness of what I want to look like. I could live with it, so I sent it on to M. Next time we talked, he started to push things farther:

23:32 pst: I bet a phone call to the UK costs a fortune

07:32 gmt: it would show up on your phone bill

23:33 pst: oh

23:34 pst: but, how much do you think it would cost?

07:35 gmt: the timing would have to be right

23:35 pst: so right, I agree

I was thinking of my husband, his wife – already the consideration of secret lovers. It turned out he was thinking of the time difference. We both let it go for a while. But something had changed, I felt it straight away and it was to do with pace. It was the first conversation we ever had that was slow. Usually we spoke so fast that nothing ever got completely answered or resolved as if we had spent our whole lives waiting to tell each other so many things. It was then that I started, I think, to know. It was then that I stopped shopping in bulk and started to go twice a day to the supermarkets in the car by myself, so that I could listen to pop music and think of things that we still hadn't said. It was then that I began to think of M in the middle of my nights. Lying next to my husband, trying to go to sleep. Only thoughts of M could relax me. Fantasies of M. M who I hadn't seen, whose voice I hadn't heard. M who was essentially letters typed individually onto a screen became the man of my dreams.

The kindergarten area is exactly the same. He reminds me that it hasn't changed in thirty-something years. But he doesn't remember that the six year olds also had their classrooms in the same square, so I remind him of that. Then I say there used to be a sandpit in the middle, where the climbing frame is now, and his face remembers that it is part of our ongoing repartee for him to correct my English nouns into American ones.

'Sandbox,' he says and I think for the first time he smiles wide enough for me to see that his teeth are so typically American: perfectly straight and as white and clean as his car.

Then he adds, 'Jungle gym.'

'What?' I say, this is beginning to reflect one of our virtual conversations and I like it that the language is becoming more familiar.

'You said climbing frame, but we natives call it a jungle gym. Don't worry you'll get the hang of the lingo before too long.'

Now my grin is so wide he can probably see my yellowed English teeth.

I was dreaming about M. The things we hadn't yet talked about; the funny stories I had yet to tell him. Sometimes I just remembered the things that we had said to each other. Stupid things:

06:42 gmt: oh I am defineatly going to see Lost in Translation when it finally comes to London

20:42 pst: definitely

06:42 gmt: what?

06:43 gmt: yes, defenitly

20:43 pst: yes you should do that - definitely see that film

20:43pst: and you should definitely learn to spell definitely

06:43 gmt: oh ha ha, so smug and perfect.

20:43 pst: I know.

20:45 pst: uh oh, have I hurt your feelings now?

06:45 gmt: so were you THAT kid?

20:45 pst: which kid?

06:46 gmt: you know, THAT kid?

20:46 pst: I will be whatever kid that you want me to be ;)

06:46 gmt: sure you will, but I was thinking of THAT kid who won all the spelling bees. Always the last one left standing with a silly righteous grin on his face?

20:46 pst: yes I admit that was me. lol

06:47 gmt: I won a spelling bee once too. Bet you don't believe that.

20:47 pst: you're right, I don't believe it. Got any proof. A certificate?

06:47 gmt: no, no certificates, but I can prove it.

06:47 gmt: go on ask me to spell any word

20:48 pst: oh ha ha ha. well done, you nearly got me.

Honestly that was the way my mind was thinking. Remembering conversations. Planning others. I thought I could tell him anything, but honestly (and honesty is something you really have to trust in this situation). I never thought I would tell him about the fantasies I was having. And I had no idea that he was having any of his own. Honestly, I didn't know.

The classrooms look the same and he remembers them all. Second grade, third, fourth, fifth, sixth. I left sometime in the sixth grade. I don't remember walking out of the class for the last time, but I do remember crying all the way to England on the plane: I don't want to emigrate, I don't want to emigrate. Must have been hell for my parents. I was never a cute little kid; always complicated and contrary. My mother still tells me that I was never helpful.

But now I am being cute and trying all the doors. Of course they are all locked – and it's a good thing they are all locked. What would we do alone in a room with each other?

It happened like this: it was a Tuesday morning. I will always think of it as a dreary north London morning in December; of course it was a Monday night for him in Southern California. I wondered if it was because I was cold or if it was because he was lonely. But it wasn't planned and I certainly never thought about it before, but somehow we found ourselves in the shower together. Must have spent two hours there. In real life we would have puckered up and at least in Britain we would have run out of hot water. I can't even remember much of the detail, but I can remember that he made me feel as if I had a beautiful secret for days afterward and that I was loved and glowing. It had to be our secret and I am glad it was; no one would ever believe me if I said how good things could be in cyberspace.

We spend a lot of time looking at the playground.

'I hated handball,' he says, 'and tetherball.'

'Tetherball was annoying; the rope always tangled and there wasn't a point to it,' I add to make him feel better. My husband is a keen sportsman – would never admit to disliking anything to do with a ball.

'It's much bigger than I remember it.'

'What is?' he says.

'The playground.'

'The yard, you mean?'

We're still walking and we come to the pavilion where we used to sit and have our sandwiches. Even the tables haven't moved, they're in the same semi-circle as they always were. I can see where the third graders sat, where they still might sit. I can smell peanut butter and jelly and bananas and thermoses of apple juice and the way our plastic lunch boxes smelled piled on each table ready for collection at the end of each day. There was never hot food.

'Hmmm, funny,' I say,' you would never find a school in Britain without a dinner hall.'

'A cafeteria, you mean.'

'Yes,' I say, it's easier not to argue with him about this. It's kind of his thing. He thinks it's "our thing" but it's really not. Not here and not now, anyway. Here and now, it's kind of annoying.

'But,' I add, 'we had hotdog day.'

'What?

'Hotdog Day. On Wednesdays. You must remember Hotdog Day. It was the highlight of the week. The PTA

used to organise a rota of mothers and every Wednesday, we used to have hot dogs. But not out here, we used to have them in the auditorium. Over there.'

The auditorium. It was across the playground, towards the rear entrance of the school. We both turn at the same time towards where we know it will be. And he says:

'Did they know we were coming or what, the door is open.'

We cross over the yellow lines for four-square and hop-scotch. We don't even comment on them. He's taking much bigger steps now. He's striding towards the open door of the auditorium – and I remember now everything we used to do there, eat hotdogs, give Christmas concerts, square dance with boys. I think how once upon a time I must have held M's hand.

After the shower, we did it in his bed, in my bed, over a piano, on a plane and on several chairs. Each time was different, but never as good as that first wet, soapy morning. And just as it never got better, it also became more frustrating. And then one of us (I like to think it was him first, but it may well have been me) brought love into it. Not just a little bit of love – a lot of it. Every day I love yous floated back and forth between us. And I miss yous, I need yous. I'm longing for yous. It went on like that for months and months. That's what finally did it for me. I knew that shopping in north London was no longer enough; I had to go back to California and check out what was on offer there. The girls, my husband – once I was on the plane I almost forgot them.

For a few minutes there is magic in the auditorium. From the moment that we leave the bright, warm morning outside and enter, I feel the craziness of it all. How we've walked all the way around the school and stood in the playground staring. No one has talked to us; asked us what we wanted with this place. And now we are in here. The only light comes in the door with us, but we can see the stage and the way the curtains fall dramatically to the sides of it. And the dance floor in front of the stage where we attended scout meetings, and spent our rainy days. And where our mothers prepared hotdogs for us every Wednesday. I take a breath and smell the mustard and when I close my eyes I can see rows of women in aprons serving us and stopping to gossip with each other. I remember how I always wanted more than one, but that was all we got. With my eyes closed it's easier to put the man I am with right now with the man I have been talking to for over a year; the man who has been telling me that he's in love with me. Just as I think that I will not be brave enough to open my eyes again, I do. M is looking at the rows of seats beyond the dance floor where we used to sit class by class and listen to the teachers or Mrs McIntyre speak to us. Maybe he is remembering the way our parents sat in those seats watching and crying a little as we sang to them from the stage every Christmas.

Once, just before I left the country, we did a talent show in here. M doesn't remember.

'I was Charlie Brown in a skit,' I tell him.

He laughs and says , 'I love your voice.'

And for that last magic moment, I feel myself melt into the words just like I do at home in London sitting with my laptop at 6 in the morning, trying to type quietly.

But then his voice squeaks a little as he says: Would you like to kiss me?

I heard myself say it, though I couldn't quite believe how I answered the question. I was typically English and polite. No, thank you, I said, and he did not ask again or even look for a reason. I don't remember much else, but somehow we made it out of the auditorium and out of the school. We did not hug when we parted. We said good-bye quickly and I didn't touch his twig-like arm again.

Of course I thought about it all the time as I continued my short tour of the place where I was born; and then on the aeroplane going home to my husband and children, and for many hours and days after I returned. In the middle of the night, during working hours, when I was cleaning and cooking and doing all those things that 41-year-old women do. And I could only come up with this: M in the shower, in his bed, in my bed, on a plane, over a piano and on several chairs does not have to ask.

I know I will never see him again. But we have what we have:

00:08 pst: You looked fantastic.

08:08 gmt: So did you. Everything I expected you to be, you were.

00:08 pst: Send me a new picture of you.

08:09 gmt: no, you send one of you.

00:09 pst: I will

00:11 pst: if you will.

08:11 gmt: you first

08:11 gmt: oh this is silly.

00:11 pst: then just say yes

00:11 pst: you know, by now, that it's easier if you do everything I ask of you.

08:12 gmt: okay, I will do anything you ask of me. Your wish is my command.

00:12 pst: good. That's the best way. I'll look for the picture tomorrow and then I will think of some new commands.

00:14 pst: but now I have to get some sleep. I love you.

08:14 gmt: sweet dreams. Me too. I miss you so much, it hurts.

00:14 pst: me too. I'm longing to see you again. talk to you tomorrow (your today)

00:14 gmt: x

08:14 pst: xo

<signed off>

And so he goes to sleep. And so I go to the shops – Tesco, Sainsbury, Asda. Nothing really changes; I always want something.

Nice Looking Boy

The boy looked nice. He smiled at me when I walked into the restaurant. Full lips set in a small mouth. Tiny nose for a boy, I thought. Rachel smiled at me too. She mirrored his look. I noticed it almost first, the way she and the boy looked more alike than her and I do.

'We can't eat anything here, Mum,' she said to me when I got to the middle of the dining room. She was carrying her necessities: mobile phone and lip gloss.

Then she kissed me on both cheeks. French style. Something new. Was this for the boy's benefit?

'How are you? Did you miss me? Can I put these in your bag?' she said putting her things into my bag.

'Good, yes and yes,' I said looking at the boy. 'Where's Allison? I want to meet her and buy her lunch too. I should thank her for letting you stay at her house last night.'

Then looking for eye contact with the boy, I said, 'Hi Jay.'

Rachel gave the coffee shop another quick scan, 'Ali had to go somewhere. Can we go somewhere?'

The boy nodded at me and kept smiling.

'Okay, we'll go,' I said. 'You two lead and I will follow.'

They led me to Pizza Express, as I knew they

would. I also knew that The Ivy at Howell's of Cardiff wouldn't be their scene, but it was an easy place for us to meet. I thought that they wouldn't really expect me to follow behind, but they did, or to be fair to them and more accurate, they made no attempt to wait for me to catch up as they walked quickly up St Mary Street towards the Castle. Nor did they turn their faces to include me in their conversation.

The young waiter laughed at a silly comment I made about being last but not least and the one with the credit card when he led us to our table. The joke was intended for Jay to show him how easy this was going to be. But the waiter seemed to like it more because he grinned at me throughout our meal as if he never had a customer speak her thoughts out loud before or maybe he thought the credit card crack meant he was up for a big tip. Jay just looked unsure and, I think, a little bit scared.

'Everyone laughs at her,' Rachel tried to explain to him, 'and she thinks she's sooooo funny.'

'I am funny, honey.' I twiddled my left earring. Yesterday we made an agreement to play with our ears if either of us mentions anything the other one of us doesn't want to talk about in front of Jay.

'Yes, Mother, but we're not laughing with you, we are laughing at you.'

I catch Jay looking from one to the other of us trying to make it out. Am I going to be angry for that comment? Or is this our mother/daughter in-front-of-boy-she's-trying-to-impress banter? He seems to decide that it is whatever it is and begins to study the pizza selection on the menu intently. I pretend to do the same, though I know that I am going for the Caesar Salad.

'Jay's going away tomorrow,' Rachel says. She will have a plain cheese pizza and ask if it can be served with ketchup. She will eat the cheese off the top of it and the soft bit from the middle but leave all of the crust. And her messy plate at the end of the meal won't at all embarrass her.

'Are you, Jay? Where are you going?' I ask, though I already know. Rachel told me that he is going with five older boys to Ibiza.

'To Italy,' he grins. And he looks at me. Straight in the eyes.

'Oh how wonderful. A family holiday?'

'Yes, my parents are taking my little brother and me. My sister isn't going though. She's staying in Cardiff with a friend so that she can keep her summer job.'

'How old is your sister?'

'She's 17.'

'So you've got the one sister? You're 15? And how old is your younger brother?' I am pretending like I need to get it all straight. I pretend like I am interested in the construction of this boy's family, when all I am really interested in is how he constructs lies and more importantly whether or not my daughter is ever in collusion with him.

Rachel plays with her earring. She is embarrassed. She knows I hate liars.

When the grinning waiter takes our order, he notices how beautiful Rachel is. I am not being a proud mother now; Rachel really is beautiful. It still surprises me sometimes to look at her. She has olive skin, which is nearly always flawless, and the kind of hair I would have killed for when I was 15. It's thick and shiny with a bit of a curl, but none of that awful frizz which I have had to battle with every day. She usually wears her hair up in a constructed sloppy bun, but a wayward curl always manages to escape down her neck to make her look vulnerable and un-self-conscious. Her best feature, most people think, are her eyes. They are the most unusual combination of grey and green. She knows how to make the best of them and nearly everyone she meets comments.

But it's that escaped fluff of hair at the back of her neck that does it for me. It reminds me of what she smelled like as a baby and the baths we used to take together and those mornings when she was 5 or 6 when she crawled into bed at dawn and woke me up singing 'Good King Wenceslas' though it was July. That bit of hair and the way it falls on that part of her neck reminds me that it was only six months ago when we talked about love and trust and how we were strangely still best friends. Now it's there, lying on her neck in the perfect shape of an upside down question mark.

When Rachel orders her margarita pizza, the waiter says, 'Wow, you have a-maz-ing eyes.' Jay and Rachel look at each other and dissolve. The laughter brings their heads closer together and the waiter and I are totally left out.

'They'll be fine once they've eaten. How long will you be away for? Don't leave me alone here with them for too long please, ' I say, trying to sound dry and serious, but the waiter and Rachel know it is another of my little quips. She rolls those beautiful eyes at me.

While we wait for our food to arrive, Jay and I have one of those conversations, which makes me wonder again what I was doing. I'd shaved my legs and put nail polish on to my toes so I could wear my highest sandals and give an impression of sophisticated confidence because Rachel is seeing a boy that she won't bring to our house. I'd plucked my eyebrows, phoned in sick to work and was sitting in a pizza restaurant on a Monday afternoon in order to understand why she needs to make elaborate and complex plans and secretive telephone calls in order to be with him. And God how I am hoping I'm wrong, but I have been putting two and two together and coming up with a whole bunch of uneasy changes that we aren't ready for. That's why I am doing this and that's why I am here. Our conversation, if you could call it that, goes something like this:

'So Jay, are you back in school as soon as you return from your holiday?'

'Yes.'

and this:

'So you'll be doing your GCSEs next year like Rachel?'

'Yes.'

and this

'And then do you think you'd like to do some A-levels and go on to university?'

'Yes.'

In between these questions there are long pauses while I wait for some elaboration, but it's just like

Oprah having a bad day. I find myself tapping on the table and looking around the dining room. Is there anyone here I know? Someone friendly and mature? Someone I could greet and speak to? Maybe I could explain this strange situation to them: Hi there. How are you? Yes, just taking my daughter and her friend to lunch. I haven't met him before as he lives on the other side of town. She always has to meet him somewhere, so I thought I should take a look. See if he's the kind of boy I can trust with her. She says he is, but you know how headstrong teenage girls can be. And I have been worried, oh how worried.

But there isn't anyone else to focus on so I take notice of the paintings on the wall instead. They are small and modern. Each picture is of a single thick brushstroke in a bright colour slashed across the canvas. So simple. So incomprehensible.

I am trying to think of another question when I notice Rachel fiddling with her ear again. Though, I think by now she had forgotten that it is supposed to mean something, I stop myself anyway.

One thing you can say for Pizza Express – it does what it says it will and the grinning waiter brought our food quickly. Sometimes you need something to focus on.

Jay and Rachel began to saw their pizzas in half in such an aggressive but unconsciously similar manner, that it was noticeable and laughable. To all of us. At last, a joke that we could share. We ate. We talked a little more. Things got a little better.

When we were done. Jay stretched himself out the

way he might do after a meal at home. He smiled genuinely at me, said thank you and his hand reached out toward Rachel. He rested his arm on her shoulder and began to play with that petulant curl lying innocently on the back of her neck.

I think a mother should know when her time's up. I paid the bill and left them at the table after thanking them for their company and arranging to meet Rachel in an hour so that I could take her home. At that point, I'm sure that I didn't remember that I still had her things in my bag.

I walked down St Mary Street and through the Hayes too unsettled for some reason to shop. There was something wrong and by the time I realised what I had done, it would have been too late to run back to Pizza Express. I wouldn't have found her. And she would already be angry and worried that I might read her text messages or that I might answer the phone. On Queen Street, it was hard not to shout out loud in praise of the new Starbucks. I sat there with mocha and someone else's discarded Daily Express, trying to focus on the news from Iraq, but wondering if the phone in my bag were password protected. The first time it started to vibrate and ring, I ignored it in an honourable way. But I only had to wait another minute before it rang again. It was easy to tell myself that it might even be her when I answered it.

'Hello, Rach?' a voice was saying.

'No, it's her mother. Who is it please?'

'Um, it's Ali, can you tell...'

'Oh right Allison,' I said, 'hey you've been a great

friend, having her to stay so much, lately. I really want you to tell your Mom thanks from me. Okay?'

'Um. Oh yeah,' she said, 'Oh sure, it's fine. I have to go now. Bye.'

She hung up and there was nothing else I needed to know.

Tattoo

Bobby's dad, Joe, had a tattoo on his arm in a time and place when people's fathers didn't have tattoos. I never saw it myself, but Bobby's parents had a swimming pool in their backyard in Pacoima and some of the other kids told me they'd seen it when they'd been out there swimming and Joe was maybe cleaning leaves from the pool or stoking up the barbeque.

Bobby's parents were the best parents I knew. I called them by their first names – Bianka and Joe – and they let Bobby decorate his bedroom by letting him paint psychedelic patterns on the wall. Bianka bought him the paint and tiny brushes so he could be precise. They also bought him the best sound system that money could buy, with the biggest speakers any of us had ever seen – and we listened to Jethro Tull and Led Zeppelin and every other band of the time. Bobby taught me about music while we painted intricate circular patterns in purples, orange, pink and sky blue on creamy walls.

Now that I think of it, Bobby's dad may have been more careful in front of me, for though I swam in that pool many times, I never remember seeing his arms or the tattoo. He thought I was Bobby's girlfriend and there was shyness about him. I stayed at the Ehrlich house even though it was a time when girls didn't stay at boys' houses. Things were so bad in my own home – the two-bedroom apartment my parents moved to when they lost our house in an economic decline. Not a depression – my dad used to say – a recession. All I knew was that he didn't have a job and my mother used to throw things at him: ornaments they'd had as wedding presents; bills in thick, brown envelopes; knives and forks; bottles of ketchup. I would hear her loud, high-pitched hysteria and, whether I stayed in the apartment with them or not, my ears rang with her bitterness. So I used to hide at Bobby's letting his music and the kindness of his parents drown out the ugly words, the horrible sounds.

I went there for lunch and stayed for dinner. Most of the time, Bianka drove me home at night. The food smelled different from the food in the apartment. It was European and Yiddish: chopped liver; kugel, latkes and knisnishs. Kasha and chicken soup with rice. It was good, so good. Bianka tried to teach me to cook, while Bobby went back into his room and painted more swirls on the wall and listened to obscure music imported from England. I never wanted to go home and so some nights, sensing my reluctance, she made up a spare bed for me – in the opposite end of the house to where Bobby was sleeping.

It didn't matter what our relationship was or wasn't. It was a time when people were more careful about such things. I thought I loved Bobby and I waited for him to love me too. I look back now and see that we were best friends and that what I was in love with was his family. And that by letting me into their lives, they rescued me. Bobby's mom died a few years later when we were in college. Bobby was at the University of Montana by then and I was still home at CSUN, the only place I could afford to be with the help of a tiny scholarship for being on the girls' track team. Bianka had breast cancer at a time when you didn't survive from it and you didn't talk about it. So when I heard about her death, it was unexpected and it shocked me. I couldn't reach Bobby in Missoula so I went to the track and ran for 45 minutes. Running and crying, running and crying.

I heard that Joe kind of went nuts after that. He sold the house, gave Bobby a wad of money and went back to Germany and married someone else very quickly. Bobby did a lot of drugs, lived alone for a long time and then he died of AIDS when we were 26.

The last time I saw him he told me that his mother loved me the best of all the friends that hung around their house and used the swimming pool. He said those words: *she loved you best,* and though I probably already knew the truth in it, it was good to be told. Bianka wanted him to take me to the prom, to rescue me from the sad rage in my own parents' home. She wanted other things for him too and he told me that she made him promise, before she sent him up north so that he wouldn't see her die, that he and I would have her grandchildren.

That day he explained to me what it was like to be the child of survivors. How he felt he could never tell them he was gay. He told me that his father told him, only once, the story of how he got the tattoo: other Jews had held him down and branded him; how the Gestapo watched and laughed when he cried – eight years old and completely alone. He told me that even when Joe told him the story of his desperate escape from the camp (how they hid in a German forest and later in a sympathetic attic) Bobby knew that he couldn't live up to that kind of heroism and believed he had no right to confide his own small confusion.

That day I finally understood. He thanked me for being his alibi for all those years when we were high school kids and I thanked him for being my rescuer. We kissed the only kiss we would ever share and held hands for a while and then a nurse asked me if I would please go now and let the patient rest.

Ordering the Wine

There are empty spaces on the shelves by Sunday. I put it off, though, that last job of the old week and the first of the new. It should be a pleasure checking how much wine's been sold – deciding what to order next, what to promote. And it is once I'm there. Once I've put my hair up, sketched some lipstick over my mouth, got into the black Astra and driven to the store, often through rain and strong winds. The way in which the clouds roll in from the sea make me think of a speeded-up time sequence in a very modern film. It's only two and a half miles or so, through the countryside. Farms, cows, a pub, a church, then the yellow store surrounded by nothing, but so important to four nearby villages who have lost their own shops, had their post offices taken away.

When I get there, my heart falls a little if there aren't six or seven cars parked out the front, if there aren't several customers with filled wire baskets wandering about, if the staff aren't busy taking money at the cash registers, if that lottery machine isn't making its distinctive de de de dede noise. Despite the fact that I am not meant to be doing this job. Never was.

I try not to catch too many eyes, because they all know me. Want to talk. Tell me about their cats: lost or died or had kittens. Tell me about the grandchildren coming to visit and how they'll want home-made Welsh cakes when they arrive. How they can't serve just any wine with lunch to their returning grown up children. Need to impress. No Liebfraumilch or Lambrusco nowadays. What kind of Merlot is on offer today? A Californian, or maybe something from Argentina?

The Chardonnays still sell pretty well, but, nowadays, people buy according to country. Napa Valley out-sells the Loire. People like the warmth of it, the distance that it's travelled and the price easily competes. South Africa appeals to me more than Australia so I stock more varieties. It's my little bit of power. My way to show personal support for a country I want to visit someday. A couple of Sauvignons, a Chenin Blanc. Something with bubbles, but nothing too sweet. The affluent farmers and city professionals on this outside edge of Cardiff have developed a sophisticated palate.

The reds are easier for me to choose. My favourite right now is a ruby Cabernet from Chile. I go through phases: there was the winter of the French Lanquedoc; autumn, though, usually demands a return to the mild-mannered Merlots from Spain.

It doesn't take long to decide what to order once I get started. And Dave is at my shoulder waiting to scan it through.

Dave knows just what to do. Scan the special offers into the machine first. Then add those items to the main part of the order. He will attach it to the computer for me. Send it all down the line as we say in the trade. I marvel at how modern we have become. Not like all those years ago when my grandfather built the store. In those days, he sold petrol and repaired farm machinery at the back, in his spare time – besides running the shop. Spare time! I remember my grandmother counting every penny in the evening. Crawling on the lino over by the broken biscuits to look for a shilling. Never more than tuppence out. But now, ten minutes and the whole order – £11,000 worth will be relayed over the phone lines to the main depot. As if by magic the goods will arrive tomorrow. Picked, packed and checked. And that's it for this week. Done and dusted, I will say. And Dave will chuckle because I say the same thing every week. Then I will ask him if he'd like me to make him some tea or coffee and I will linger checking the bread dates, the stock levels of the cigarettes, secretly surveying the uniform and dirty fingernails of the staff on the tills. Not really wanting to leave, even though I could. Go home, back to the papers, to the half-cooked dinner, or to arrange a game of squash at the club.

It's when I hand the order book to Dave, and start to give him the same instructions he hears every week, that I catch something of Jesse. A certain look in the eye? Or the way a hand reaches for the scanner? Maybe it's just the preciseness of doing the exact same thing at the same time every week; but something stops, and I remember her.

Just a moment, but in it I remember the smell of her hair. She used cheap stuff, but it smelled of vanilla or wild blossom. No matter where she'd been the night before it was always clean when she came in. I remember her eyes; enormous and blue. The way they could fill up in response to a customer or co-worker's sad story: a dead animal; a sick child; a dying parent. A stolen car, even. And I remember the way she bounced into the store, turning everything on its head. Hey Dee, where do you want me today? Sorry I'm late; the bus didn't stop for me. Had to get a taxi. Oh and it took ages, walked all the way into town. But I'm here now. No problem, right? Till, is it? Or do you want me to clean out that dairy cabinet? I can do that for you, of course I can.

Customers loved her – ask about her still, *Do you hear from that girl, you know the loud pretty one. I loved her.* She told them her background was Irish, Italian, Navajo. Whatever they wanted to hear.

Oh yes, she knew people: what they wanted and what they could be like. How to play them. Learned it first hand. Parents who couldn't get it right, didn't try. You learn to adapt when you're moving all over the place. It came out in fragments, her story. St Louis to South Carolina and then to Scotland via Dublin. Lots of schools but sometimes not allowed to go. Lots of accents, too, always trying to fit into the locality. Her dad was brilliant, but something about him not quite right. He went from university course to university course, but couldn't be left alone, so sometimes Jesse had to stay up with him until he was ready to fall asleep. Maybe three or four in the morning. A kid thinks everyone else's dad is like that. Her mother out working nights making something for them to live on. Now her mother has moved down here to Cardiff and is trying to make a new life with a man she met on a long distance train. A confirmed bachelor who never thought he might have to share his bay view flat with a 17-year-old from another continent. Still, what could he do? His new wife from Edinburgh, Dublin and St Louis was pregnant and he never thought this chance for so much happiness would come his way. Not now. Not at his age. So he told her straight. As soon as the baby is born, Jesse has to go. There are places for young girls and she'll have to find one. There's money out there too. It's hardly a surprise.

Jesse knows she's not wanted in their love nest and can't go back to her dad. Though he phones and begs her to, sometimes, when he thinks of it. But she can't get the last view she had of him out of her head. Lying face down on the bathroom floor in his own vomit trying to win over the sympathy of his deserting wife. Jesse, alone, had spent that whole night trying to knock down the locked door. She could hear him behind it, emptying all the tablets from their containers, Lithium and Prozac and Valium. He added aspirin and Benilyn for good measure. She heard when he finally fell – he was 19 stone after all. She could smell him, she could visualise him, she could hear him, but she couldn't get the door open. Not until she finally stopped sobbing long enough to remember the police. She called them. They broke down the door. Mostly she remembers their black boots on the grey tiles and her father's stinking body being turned over with rough uncaring hands.

For us to get to that point, for her to confide, she

had to know something about me. It was only fair. A little snippet of Jesse's life – the time her father tied her mother to a chair with his leather belt – was answered with a little snippet from mine: six infertility treatments in ten years and the reason I won't be having babies. Or the story about when Jesse was eight and got nits and her mother shaved her hair off completely in the old-fashioned way and it was the one term she insisted on taking Jesse into school. Her purple woollen hat wasn't allowed in the classroom. I tried to match this with the confession that when I was her age, I'd have liked to apply to art school, but, as an only child whose mother and father were also only children, our traditional family business was my responsibility. Keeping it going was the only way for my parents to have a retirement. I remember telling Jesse that I had no choices,

She must have thought some of the things I told her were stupid and petty. After all, my disappointments were punctuated by country club membership, a house surrounded by fields, a husband who loved me no matter what and enough money. But she didn't say. She understood in an 18-year-old-ancient-as-the-Gods way. In return, I tried to understand her too, not just be shocked by all that can go on.

There were funny moments. The way she wouldn't let little things get in the way. Once a customer called me a truly terrible name because his lottery ticket got stuck in the machine. When he left, I turned to her, tearful and frustrated, as angry as I've ever been, and said, Can you believe he called me THAT? And she said don't worry, Dee, someone calls me a twat every single day of my life.

It was the way she made it funny and the way her eyes would widen and the way she thought I was someone she could trust that took it beyond any relationship I've had with anyone.

I arranged her shifts around her college hours and made sure I could be there too. I was supposed to be dealing with reps, ordering stock, hiring and making decisions, but we talked and gossiped, the way I never intend to.

My squash-playing friends said, 'Don't get involved.'

My husband, the teacher, said, 'You're getting involved.'

But they were wrong. I was already involved. Too late.

Sometimes she asked for things on tick. *I'll pay you at the end of the week.* Something to eat maybe, I'd seen how thin she was getting. I tried not to notice that it was whisky and cigarettes she borrowed.

'Where are you going to live?' I said.

'I don't know, I don't know.'

Once I said to her, Maybe I could talk to them, your mother and her man. Maybe they don't realise you're thinking of giving up college. That you don't have anywhere to go. But she'd reassure me, No worries, I can stay at Richard's/Rob's/Michael's. No worries.

But I worried.

My husband tells me that things started to go

downhill then. He pointed out that she was always letting me down at the last minute and the excuses were more and more elaborate and that usually it was me making the excuses. She's late because she lost her shoes. She can't come in because she's looking for a particular dye for a project. She's really sorry, though; said she would make it up next time. She'll come in earlier, defrost the freezer. Help with the order.

And I would give up a game of squash or a night at the cinema to go and do her shift, cover for her, thinking I was doing something good. Something to help her.

My squash-club friends were incredulous. They said, 'She must be lying to you.'

My husband said, 'She's lying and you're letting her. If she can lie to you what else is she capable of?'

No no no.

He could see I was never going to believe it. He thought that being friendly to customers all the time, controlling things, getting up all those mornings to sort out newspapers and staying open late to sell all that wine was impairing my judgement. He wanted to help more, but I wouldn't let him. Planning geography classes at advanced level is stressful enough, I'd say. The truth is I didn't want him there. Jesse and I and the others were coping. *We're coping just fine.* But he told me that in the August holiday we were going to have a break.

'We can explore the Napa Valley,' he said. 'See all those little vineyards you're always reading about. Do some serious wine tasting. Maybe we could camp in

Yosemite, we always said we would one day.'

It was tempting. It was very tempting, but how could I leave my store. How could I? And Jesse? Her mother's baby due any day.

And then it came to me.

'I'll do it,' said Jesse, when I asked her. I'd offered her everything. Stay in our house. Use the car. I could pay for her insurance for a few weeks because after all she would be doing me a huge favour, looking after things, making sure the others turned up on time, locking up.

'No worries,' she said, 'I'll do it.'

But my husband didn't see it that way. He told me he'd take care of it. I let him. It was odd, but I let him.

'Dave would be the perfect choice,' he said. 'Dave doesn't want to stay in our home. Dave doesn't need our car. Dave knows the job inside out and backwards. Dave's never late, or absent. He doesn't have huge problems. And above all he doesn't lie.'

She took it really well. After my husband settled our plans with Dave, I wanted to be the one to tell her. I guessed that all those disappointments she'd already had in her life made this seem a very small thing.

'No worries. I understand,' she said.

'I need to ask you to please be on time for Dave while I am away and to help him if you can, especially at first,' I said. 'And if you need time off, will you get it covered by one of the others?'

Maybe I'd said too much, but I didn't think so at the time. She laughed it off in that way of hers and her eyes got bigger and then turned serious. You can trust me, Dee, you know you can. Just go, she said, Just go and have a wonderful time.

I remember how I planned that trip out loud with Jesse in the store. Sometimes, I wonder if I talked about it more with her than I did with my husband. I told her about the route we would take up Pacific Coast Highway, stopping in Santa Barbara, St Luis Obispo. Hearst Castle. She told me about America: how easy the driving would be; things we should eat. She told me that the Americans would love my accent and give us extra French fries with everything.

It was just like that too. The most wonderful three weeks I'd ever had. It was better than French fries with everything; we saw the busiest, noisiest ocean, violent waves crashing upon one another. We met people who would do anything for us just as long as we spoke to them about Wales in our Welsh accents. We watched the most romantic sunsets. The wine tasted like walnuts and oak and the sea. In that time, I forgot everything I was supposed to worry about: the store, and my parents relying on my good sense and that our family would always be just us – my husband and I.

Dave knew how to reach us, but he didn't. Not once.

Afterwards, I asked why he hadn't phoned. He said, 'What could you have done? We managed. We got through it.'

I gave him a bonus. Even bigger than the bonus I had planned to give him. I also gave him the two bottles of Matilija Springs Pinot Grigio. The one that

was for him and the one that should have been
Jesse's.

He told me that Jesse had been there the first day
of our vacation. She seemed so anxious to help. She
scoured the stock room and did the snacks and
chocolate order for him. She wasn't late that day and
she didn't ask for time off or try to change a shift. She
didn't borrow anything and even paid off what she
owed in the book. She was excellent. Dave had been
relieved, but when he counted the money at the end of
the night some of it was missing. A lot of it, actually.

'I panicked,' he said, 'but not for long.'

In the drawer amongst the coupons and credit card
receipts he found a note:

*Wages taken: £400 for three weeks in advance.
Jesse.*

'I could have dealt with that,' Dave said, 'only she
never turned up again. We tried to phone. But she
doesn't live with her mother any more.'

When I remember this part of the story, what I see is
not Jesse taking money that wasn't hers to take and
leaving the store and Dave without a look back or a
thought for what she and I had shared. What I see is
my husband's look when I told him. The way he shook
his head. The way he pitied me for being so bad at
knowing who to trust. The way he would not listen to
me when I defended her for only taking what was
rightly or wrongly hers. Teachers, I find, think in
black and white. This one, he says, is a liar, a bad girl.
He thinks that, now, I would know her for what she
is. That I would not speak to her if she returned to the

scene of the crime.

But I would. Oh I would. I would ask her forgiveness.

Spirals

There was only a little wind and John was not at home. The right timing. Fall, or as they call it here, Autumn. Early November: the sky showing a bit of blue. No rain for a change, and even so, the temperature had dropped only a few degrees. It was difficult to remember that soon it would be colder. So cold sometimes that getting undressed for bed would mean putting the same amount of clothing back on: long sleeved t-shirt; leggings; thick socks.

In the garden, Nat picked at the dead heads on the pansies for a while. This will do, she thought. The garden was spacious and private like the house. Their neighbours in the field next door were six heifers. From the other side of the stone wall, she could hear their grazing noises. They would live here as long as there was still enough grass to feed off before they were slaughtered. The farmer told Nat once that they were not cows, but heifers – young and female, they would not be allowed to mature, just to get fatter and fatter and then they would be killed. John advised her not to think about it. It was, after all, the way of life and something that she would need to accept if she was going to make her life in this place. Accept the rituals of farmers. Today, though, the cows would be her only witnesses.

It would be good to settle now. Finally after years of being here, but looking for something else. Someone? Wondering whether anywhere else would be better. Or just different? It was time to accept what life had brought and settle down to it. John, of course, had always been settled. And soon they would have a child.

The thought of the baby made Nat smile. She hoped the baby would keep her warm over the winter and when it was born next spring focus her mind on the house and the garden and on John. Stop looking. She always seemed to be reminding herself not to look forward or backward or anywhere else. She was here. It was decided. But first, before she could tell John that he was right after all, she needed to get everything straight. She looked around her again. The cows, the quiet house, the lonely garden. Only the cows.

Nat went into the house, through the kitchen and up the stairs and into their bedroom. Of all the rooms this one smelled like John. He had a good smell; though he was fastidious there was also something vaguely sweat and socks and sporty about him, also talcum powder and Old Spice. Sometimes after a match – rugby or cricket or squash – there was menthol. The menthol mixed with the thought of their lovemaking and passed quickly through Nat's mind. And then was gone. For a moment she felt warm and comfortable and wondered why. Then, that too was gone and forgotten.

Nat wanted to get the thing done. She'd considered it often, more so recently and though she felt sure it wasn't a sign of impending death (as she always thought it would be) she knew she had to do it soon. No matter how hard it would be to get rid of. She'd waited until the right time. A good clear day, John away from the house.

To get to what she didn't want anymore, Nat had to crouch down low and almost crawl into the wardrobe and feel for the parcel she'd hidden behind her shoes and underneath a bag of old tights that she wouldn't wear again. She knew the exact location and found it easily, though she didn't think it would be easy for anyone else to find. But it was this thought, this uneasiness, that someone else might find the parcel by accident; come upon it innocently, open up the carefully folded plastic bag and then lift out one of the notebooks, flick through it and catch a word or two, a name, and then decide to read on.

The thought of that happening, no, the horror of that happening, haunted Nat and she knew what she had to do.

The notebooks were wrapped in an old carrier bag from Disneyland. Folded as it were so that Mickey Mouse's grin greeted her when she lifted the parcel from behind her shoes. If found, would John know what the parcel was? Probably. He knew that she kept a real diary full of her words, although she tried to avoid talking about them to anyone. She told him only that it was her method of dealing with things and because of the notebooks she knew exactly what was wrong with her and she would never have to see a therapist. He'd laughed at her then and said, 'Of course Natalie, you'll never need a therapist, you're about to marry one.'

Nat would turn away from him when he talked about marriage and that in itself would cause an argument or, worse, silence, but at least it got them off the subject of the notebooks. And Nat felt safe enough to continue writing it all down. For a while.

Now she didn't open the parcel. She took the bag and its contents and left the bedroom. Down the stairs more quickly now. Past John's inherited grandfather clock. She noted the time. She had perhaps forty minutes. That should do it.

In the kitchen she looked for matches. Neither of them smoked but every night in the winter John lit the fire in the dining room. Nat tried to talk him into converting the old fireplace to gas like the rest of the house, but John liked the images of the flame against the crumbling chimney breast. He liked the procedure of cleaning out the grate and laying the kindling for the fire in the mornings before his breakfast. He sat near the fireplace in the evenings, drinking wine and doing paperwork or just looking at the patterns of the flame. It was a simple picture and thinking of it Nat felt something like a rush of love for him surge through her. It surprised her. She put it down to the baby and her changing hormones. She scolded herself out loud. Stop being silly and sentimental. Get on with the job.

Armed with matches and her parcel Nat went back outside. It was such a large garden, too big for them and it looked it. Some of the borders were neat, but in other places the grass and weeds crept into cleared spaces. There was never enough time. It took an hour or so to cut the lawn and that too was never finished. The edges weren't trimmed at the same time as the lawn was mowed. There were so many trees: cherry; eucalyptus; birch. Around their base clumps of grass and rock roses grew long and wild. Nat liked them and left them on purpose, but John eventually hacked at them, hopelessly. The garden, *this* garden, would always be too big to manage this way.

In a far corner John had built a brick barbecue one summer. Like the winter-evening fires, it was part of his domestication. He thought that if they had a house and a relationship they should also have a barbecue. It didn't mean that he had to use it. Once they'd invited some of his cricket friends and their girlfriends and Nat arranged salads and warmed up bread in the kitchen between running out onto the patio to refill wine glasses and over to the barbecue to turn over and baste the meat. John's idea of entertaining was to hold court with his friends, enjoy himself and drink an unaccustomed amount of alcohol. John did not cook. Nat called this a 'man-thing' and accepted it, but she refused to barbecue again.

Now, though, it would come in handy.

She unwrapped the parcel and counted the notebooks. There were eight. Almost one for every year. Most of them were spiral bound, bought with the shopping. Nothing special, on purpose. Small. Easily hidden behind a cushion or underneath the bed. Quickly out of the way. Two of the books were larger though, more cumbersome with thick covers. Nat remembered finding them discarded in John's study.

She'd needed something to write on quickly. Couldn't wait to get to down to the Spar in the village. She'd taken them. John didn't notice.

Silly now, she put them in order. The first was one of the thick books and the first few pages were filled with John's handwriting. Quick notes for something he must have typed up later. A single black line slashed through the words. His slash, not hers. Three pages only, then her scrawl, sometimes big, always unpredictable handwriting filled the rest of the book.

Nat flicked through the pages. Each entry addressed to no one and often started 'Not much time to write but...' Still the need to.

The first book was filled with the adventure. New country, leaving home, leaving Santa Barbara, leaving my family, coming to Wales. Anxiety. Will they ever like me? And the loneliness. No one to talk to. And John so busy. Why does he want me? I'm too fat. I haven't had an appetite for three weeks, I must eat. Why doesn't he notice? I must phone home. I must learn how to bake a fruit cake like John's mother. They all want us to marry. He wants me to stay home. *Just* stay home? No he means stay home and have babies. Oh help, help this is not me.

Nat put it onto the grill of the barbecue.

The second book was calmer. By then she had a job. She'd talked him into it or had he noticed her unhappiness? She couldn't remember and the pages gave nothing away. 'I'm too tired / busy / drunk / homesick to write really, but...' There was not enough time to read all the words. Her words. Still she wanted to see once more when it had started. When

61

Guy appeared in her book. In her life. When had Guy begun to be her friend? To tease her, first, in the coffee-room. To take her to lunch. To listen to her. To talk to her, too. About his bad marriage – his horrible wife. His unhappiness. When had it begun?

There was a gap in the dates between the second book and the third. Only three months, but by then Guy's name was on every page. Their affair was the topic of books three, four and five. By the end of the fourth, she wrote about being in love with him, longing for change, not sleeping, waiting for phone calls; *he says he will leave his wife, but not yet.* And at the same time John talking more and more about marriage. Children. He says we aren't getting any younger. Don't you have a biological clock? How was she going to tell him that she'd found the person she wanted to have babies with and it wasn't him?

Now Nat threw the books (two, three, four and five) onto the grill in disgust. She lit a match and held it to the corner of one of the books. It burned a little, blackened and then the flame went out. She lit another and the same thing happened. She tried again – watched minuscule bits of one page catch and blacken before the burning stopped and the little flame died out. And then again. Another match and then another and another. She cursed her Californian childhood, the browned scorched mountains. Never the need to create warmth. Never the need to make a fire. This should be an easy task. It all should have been easier.

Nat could see her words and secrets laid out – on the grill. Ready to burn, but intact. Each book was still whole. Desperately she kept at it; lighting matches one by one and holding each to a page. Tearing the pages from the notebooks now. The words blurring through frustrated tears and she could only see his name – Guy, Guy, Guy. And she could hear her own voice: oh come on burn. Burn. Please, let it burn.

There was smoke, though still no flame and Nat smelled it on her clothes before she realized that she was choking on it and would be sick. And then was. The baby and the smoke and the time. But somehow this calmed her and she felt better. Determined. The notebooks stank. They were charred, black, curled in places and she couldn't give up; couldn't gather them together and take them back into the house, hide them away again behind her shoes. They would have to burn. No choice.

And with the next match they did. Somehow books one through five caught fire and started to burn the way she'd imagined they would, wildly and quickly. She'd imagined her sadness, maybe tears at the ending of something, the beginning of something else, but instead she felt strangely stilled and glad and – stronger. When she was certain that the fire was powerful enough, she added book six and seven without looking at them at all. In one of them she'd pasted a clipping from the company magazine. A photograph of Guy and his management team doing some important decision-making. Originally the irony of that hadn't occurred to Nat. She had kept it because she wanted a record of what he looked like. Always, even when they were so close, somehow she knew that she'd want to keep a record of him.

Only one book left to go on the flames and it would be finished. Nat added book eight, but it was too soon. The flames smothered. Smoke poured from the barbecue; the burning stopped. There were still words in view, events that must be obliterated. Nat removed the book and relit the fire, easily now. While she waited she glanced, without thinking, at the words in the final book. It was only half used. Stopped abruptly.

She had a new notebook upstairs. Not hidden. Though it was almost empty too. John had bought it for her. It was very pretty, a sweet iris on the cover. He probably bought it in a classy boutique where they sell gentle gifts. Benign presents. He knew that she liked to write things down and he wanted to show his encouragement. She felt it wrong to hide it from him so she kept it out in the open where he could see it. Sometimes she still felt the need to write things down. Take coat to cleaners. Or, Buy socks.

Nat knew what was in book eight, of course. So why did the words hit her so suddenly? And clearly through the smoke, the ash of burning books? Pregnant. Pregnant and Guy. Guy and his wife. Guy and his transfer. Me. Me and my abortion. Termination. Final. Alone. Alone. Alone. She flicked through quickly, but it was all slow motion. A stern, businesslike doctor and his kind assistant. Was she a nurse? She must have been. Hold my hand. I want my mother. Hold my hand, please. I'm thinking of getting married actually. Just not part of the plan. Not right now. You know how it is. Over so quickly. How can it be over with so quickly? An outpouring of words and pain, while I hide in our bed. Don't worry, John, it's probably just the flu. 24 hours and I will be fine.

Nat closed the book and put it in the fire with the ashes of the others.

It seemed a long time since. Waiting. The book which recorded all of it hadn't been discovered. No one found out. John trusted her. Or he wasn't curious enough. Or. What he wanted, what he'd always wanted was to marry her and have babies.

With a twig Nat sifted through the ashes to see if anything was left. No words. A low wind caught some of the thin soot and lifted it up towards the treetops. In a few minutes John would be home. She would talk to him right away. He'd waited so long and now it would be just the way he planned it. There was nothing else. Nothing left. Except some spirals, leftover binding.

Kindergarten

Row, row, row your boat...

I am the baddest girl in the kindergarten. The room smells like warm, sour milk or is that just the breath of all the rest of the children? The ones who can drink the milk and not gag it back up making a mess for Mrs Blake to clean up when she has 25 other five-year-old children to deal with here, not just you.

I'm on a mat behind the piano and it smells like socks on people's feet too long or in the laundry basket bunched up, scrunched up fresh from unfresh feet or my mommy's fingers after she's sorted through them and put them in the washing basket. That's what the mat smells like.

It's stiff brown plastic, the mat, and the edges where it folds in three to make a square for putting in the cupboard are cutting into my bare legs. And it's hot and sticky and my dress keeps moving up my thighs way too high. Mark Messer snuck his head around the piano and whispered to me, I can see the birthmark on the top of your leg, Barrie Volk, and then he scurried away in case he also ended up being punished for being bad.

gently down the stream.

Daniella Gray who's nice and lives three doors away from me on Redbush Avenue and whose father works nights so her mommy doesn't allow Daniella to play out too late also whispered to me after Mark did. She said, It's almost time to go home, Barrie, I'll walk with you. She smiled at me because she saw me crying after I threw up the milk over the side of the table and the way Mrs Blake rushed over to hold me by the elbow and lead me to the bathroom. She followed and watched while Mrs Blake wiped me down hard, hitting my chest and stomach, rubbing toilet paper over my mouth. It hurt more than last time and I couldn't stop crying, which made the corners of Mrs Blake's mouth curl upwards. Her eyes never blinked.

After milk time, Mrs Blake lets the children sing every day. She sits at the piano and plays it with her hands and feet and teaches the children songs, The wheels on the bus go round and round, round and round, or Old MacDonald had a farm. Yesterday when I was behind the piano on my mat during singing time I was trying to guess which animal would come next on MacDonald's farm. They had a duck (quack, quack here) and a cow (moo, moo there) and I guessed the next one would be a sheep, but Mrs Blake chose a horse for the last animal and it made me a little bit happier to hear all the children make horse noises and then the song was finished.

She plays the piano hard like she wants to hurt it

and she plays it for a long time, almost until home time and even though she tells me to close my eyes and try to sleep on the mat behind the piano after I've thrown up my milk, the sound of the music and singing and some laughter from the other children and the way the piano moves a little bit as she plays it keep me awake. My stomach hurts and I'm sticking to the mat and I can smell old socks and now Mark Messer has put his face around the side of the piano and stuck his tongue out at me. I am trying not to cry again. I hate Mark Messer.

merrily, merrily, merrily...

One day last week, when the milk monitor came around with the trays of milk, I said, no thank you and I sat on the benches with the other girls eating the red apple mommy gave me to have instead of the milk. We talked about why Bonnie German wears glasses on her face. She said it was because they made her smarter and we all believed her. I said I was gonna go home and ask my mommy for glasses so I could be smarter, but then Marcie Dean said that Bonnie German was lying and that glasses are only worn by children whose eyes don't work right and there was a fight. Bonnie German started to cry and Marcie Dean called her a baby – a big, fat, blind baby and Bonnie German got up from the table and pulled Marcie Dean's long brown hair. Bonnie German is the biggest girl in our class and she's the strongest and she's got the biggest hands.

From the other table, the boys were yelling, Fight!

Fight! and Mrs Blake came from inside the classroom, high heels clicking and pearly necklace bouncing and she stopped Bonnie German from hitting Marcie Dean a second time by making them both sit down on opposite sides of the table and she made the boys stop shouting by shaking her head in their direction. As she passed to go back into the kindergarten, she stopped above me and said, Barrie Volk, where is your milk?

I told her that I didn't want any today.

'You don't want the milk your mommy and daddy pay for you to have,' she said loudly. She was mad. Her eyes were big and staring.

'Get up,' she said, and she stuck her thumb and finger either side of my elbow and led me into the classroom.

'Get a mat from the cupboard,' she said, 'and get yourself behind the piano and stay there until it's time to go home.'

So now I'm on the mat and I'm listening to the children sing my favorite song. She's taught the girls and boys to sing it in a round. I can hear Bonnie German and Marcie Dean and the other girls start: *row, row, row your boat*, and when they get to *gently*, the boys start the song. The sound rolls around the room and it makes me think of how the horses on a merry-go-round are high when the one next to them is low, of how they roll and change position and the horses are colorful and rolling and moving; of how everything works together.

I move my lips along with the girls' part of the

song, but I'm not good at anything, so by the time the round is finished, I'm singing the last line with the boys:

life is but a dream.

The Tree

From the sitting room window, Susan saw Andy drive up the hill to the farmhouse. It was six-thirty, he'd be wanting his supper. She made a half turn to get to it and then stopped herself as something caught her eye. She tried to make out what he had in the back of the pick-up. In the dim evening light, it looked large and dark and worrying. Before he opened the truck's door to climb out, Susan saw him glance at their bedroom upstairs to see if she was watching him from there. Quickly she let the curtain, which had been resting on her shoulder, slide back into its place before he could catch her.

When he came through the front door a few minutes later, she was in the kitchen pretending to be busy fixing his supper. She also pretended that she did not hear him come in.

'Sue,' he called. And then again, 'Susan.'

She came into the room and looked at him. She saw that the thing in back of the pick-up had been a tree. Now it was behind him on the porch. He wanted her permission to bring it into the house.

'No,' she said.

'Aw, Sue, how long you gonna keep this up? It's nearly Christmas.'

'What did you think?' she said, but didn't wait for

him to answer. She went back to the kitchen, took his food from the microwave and put it on the table. Then she pulled her heavy fleece from the hook by the front door and went out. On the porch, she had to reach behind the tree lying on its side to get her rubber boots.

Automatically, Susan set out in the direction of what she could only refer to now as The Place. She'd been going there more often recently. Much more so than when it first happened. As the anniversary came and passed, she'd find herself going there after every silent argument she had with Andy. Often when she got to The Place, she wished for flowers or a toy and berated herself out loud for forgetting.

To get to The Place, Susan had to cross two of Andy's largest fields. In one of them, there were American Angus still grazing in the December dark evening. They did not bother her. In the next field, Andy had planted winter beans and Susan knew that she had to be careful to stick to the path.

In the sky, there was a half-moon and stars. The night was bright and beautiful like the hymn they'd had. To the south, one particularly luminous star could've been Mars or Venus. It would have been a perfect evening if only she could know that Ben was at the house sleeping in his bottom bunk. But as it happened she felt certain that nothing would be perfect or good again and this knowledge strengthened in her in the way of someone who has no expectations of fear. She heard her own hollow ironic laughter break the starry silence. Even Andy would find humor in the notion of her possessing anything remotely like strength. He would finally think I cracked completely if I told him I was strong, she thought and then her eyes filled again, her throat tightened and she tried to stop thinking about herself at all and concentrate instead on the walk and the fields. The smell. The noxious fumes getting stronger and the sound: the unsettling rumble of the highway as she got closer to the edge of the property.

Is it always like this? The house is so far from the road that it's difficult to know. Does it ever quiet down? Are there times when there's no traffic? When little animals and little people could be safe here?

She tried to imagine what Ben had smelled and heard. What was the last thing his mind registered? The same questions always: Did he cry for me? Did he call for me? How much hurt did he feel?

And also as always the anger rose. At Andy again. It was Andy who wouldn't let her see Ben's broken body. He was trying to protect her, he said, but how was it protection when he'd also told everyone else that there was no point; she would not have recognized her baby.

Even now at this time of night, late in December, the road was furious. Susan stood as still as she could, but shuddered anyway as the cars and trucks raced past her so quickly that it was hard to see that there were people in control of them. She imagined – no, she accepted – that the vehicles were nameless and faceless and in control of themselves.

When she went back to the house, Susan put Andy's empty plate into the dishwasher and cleared away the empty bottle of Southern Comfort left on the table.

Later in the week, Susan watched as Andy took the box of decorations from the basement. On the porch, he stood the tree in the same red bucket they'd been using for years. In the box, he found the wooden ornaments they'd bought for their first Christmas together. There was a Santa on skis, a reindeer with a red nose, snowmen and bells and a wooden whistle. He also found the red and white ribbons and the lights. As he worked he tried not to think of the Christmas before last when the three of them had done the job together. Susan had popped corn and she tried to show Ben how to sew the kernels together with needle and thread. Ben's baby hands were soft and plump, his fingers too clumsy. Most of the corn had broken and Ben and he ate them quickly while Susan protested in that half-serious way of hers. He remembered how she used to be when everything mattered to her so much.

Susan couldn't stop watching Andy as he worked on the tree in the porch. As he was tying on the red ribbons, she brought him a mug of coffee. She looked at him close enough to see that there were tears in his determined eyes. For a moment she touched his rough hand.

Before bed that night, Susan and Andy could see the sparkling tree through the cotton curtain as they sat together in the living room. For the first time in a while Andy did not rise from the couch halfway through a television program and leave the room to find a drink.

The next morning at breakfast, Andy asked Susan if she would like to go out with him that night. She agreed. She was feeling better; it would be good to get out.

Another question was more tentative:

'Would you like me to bring the tree into the house?'

She thought for a moment.

'Leave it where it is, just for now,' she said, but she smiled at him.

For much of that day, Andy whistled to himself as he worked around the farm. He repaired a fence and wondered if Susan might want another baby. He did. He wanted a baby so badly that he had to remind himself to slow down. So far there was only dinner and a movie to look forward to.

When they left the house that night, Andy noticed that Susan had painted her fingernails. She'd done something different with her hair.

'Could we leave the tree lights on?' she asked. 'It will be nice when we come home.'

At the restaurant they talked, carefully at first, and then Susan noticed that she was flirting. It was like when they were first married, before Ben – before anything. As he ate, she noticed his strong, square hands and his thick soft neck. Dessert lasted longer than they thought and going to a movie was forgotten. Susan realized that she was looking forward to going home with him.

In the pick-up, she put her hand on his thigh and as they drove up the hill to their house she could see the lights of the tree welcome them.

Christmas approached, Susan began to make plans. She cleaned the house top to bottom. She froze sugar cookies and made Christmas candy. She phoned some of their neighbors and invited them to come up on Christmas Eve for a few hours. No one had been to the house for over a year, yet she wasn't surprised when the kind folks around accepted her invitation easily. People are good, she thought, and she felt pretty good. She and Andy were making some kind of start.

She didn't stop thinking of Ben, though. He was always there, underlining every thought. But instead of imagining him in unimaginable pain and calling for her, she pictured a quietly spoken Ben, older than he would ever be, urging her to move on and to trust his father. This Ben was so like Andy, that it made her smile a little.

She sent for a list of local evening classes. After Christmas she would learn French. Why not?

On the Sunday morning before Christmas, Andy and Susan stayed together late in bed. They mirrored each other as they looked towards the ceiling, forgetful of the way their hips were touching slightly.

'We should bring the tree inside before Tuesday,' Susan mused, 'I guess it would make people more comfortable here.'

'I feel pretty comfortable here.'

'I know you do,' she laughed at him, but then added more seriously, 'you know what I mean.'

'Yeah, I know what you mean, honey,' Andy said. 'I'll get up and do it now.'

'Not right now, tomorrow,' Susan said, and rolled herself onto him.

The next day, Susan went into Barstow to get Andy a present. It wasn't easy to choose one considering the way they'd lived together but separately during the past year. Now though, she felt a great need to get him something special.

By the time she'd visited the department store and the bookshop and the outfitters and then decided to go back for the camera she'd seen in the first place, it was getting late. She picked up something for their supper and headed home.

As she drove up their lane, towards the house, she noticed that she couldn't see the tree in the porch window. Andy must have moved it inside already. But if he was at home, then where was the pick-up?

In the house there was no sign of Andy and though she looked room by room for the tree, she already knew that someone had taken it. There were muddy boot prints on the porch. The differing sizes made her think of a father and son. By the time Andy arrived, Susan convinced herself that the tree had been stolen for a family that couldn't afford to buy one of their own. She wouldn't let Andy call the police.

It helped her a lot to think about the family that would have their Christmas tree and their lights and ornaments. Susan pictured the family eating a poor dinner – maybe they would only have bacon and potatoes. Maybe there were lots of children – five or more – who wouldn't have stockings filled with candy cane and gifts. At least the poor family would have a tree; it would provide some kind of hope for them as it had for her and Andy just when they were more in need of hope than anything else. What did it matter if they had to take our tree? Perhaps it was all the father could do for his children. Andy and I are so much better now. Everything seems so much better now. There will be other Christmas trees.

While Susan persuaded herself of the basic honesty and neediness of her thieves, Andy seethed. He thought of the whistle and wooden baubles that he lost from the front porch. He should have brought it all in. It was careless to leave it outside where it could be seen from the road and be taken. Then he thought of how he'd lost Ben the same way. Ben had to be somewhere. He'd looked and looked for an hour or more, oblivious to the chaos that Ben's poor body was causing on the highway – the ambulance, the highway patrol, the lone Samaritan who actually stopped his car and tried to help and the faceless bastard who hadn't stopped at all. He remembered Susan's misery. The noises she made for weeks afterwards; the way she looked at him when she was quiet again.

But now Susan was almost happy. Why couldn't she see that once again someone had taken something from them? He watched and listened while Susan spent the evening talking about the fictional family who were, even now, singing carols around their tree. According to Susan, their tree was part of someone else's hope. She was creating melodrama. Couldn't she see that he'd had a stomach full? By Christ, he needed a drink. Would she ever go to bed?

When Susan woke the next morning and saw that Andy had not slept with her, she knew that she would find him drunk where she'd left him. She showered and then phoned the four families they'd invited to their Christmas Eve party. She simply said that Andy had come down with something. No apology. She thought she might have heard relief in her neighbors' voices.

Much later, when Andy woke in the sitting room, he knew that he was alone in the house. It was quiet. Then he looked at the bottles he'd emptied the night before and vomited on the stairs on the way to the bathroom.

As Susan walked through the cornfield, she noticed that someone had trampled on the path, mindless of what might be growing. Following the direction of the damage with her eyes she could make out an ominous shape against the hedge that adjoined the highway. As she walked toward it, she started to recognize some of the debris on the ground. There was a red ribbon, some wooden baubles, a whistle. By the time she came to the hedge she knew that she would find the mangled remains of their tree, strangled with its own fairy lights.

Another Las Vegas Story

It is 1951 and Michael is nearly five. Mommy and Daddy have told him to stand here on the pavement and be still. They said not to talk to any strangers when they went into Aunt Charlotte's place – the big bright storefront behind him. They said that they'd be watching him through the giant window and for him to stand right in front of it. Be still. He could see them now if he stood on his tiptoes and put his nose and his eyes right up to the glass – his mother sitting high on a stool, legs crossed in a row with some other ladies. There was a big red flower in her hair. Just her, no one else was wearing a flower. She was talking and laughing, he could tell it was her loud laugh and whenever she moved it looked like she was dancing even though she was sitting down. Some men had gathered around a long table. They were looking hard at the table and at each other and making a lot of noise. Michael could hear them through the windows.

Mommy had given him a brown bag with grapes in it and a Hershey Bar which was now in his pocket. Yesterday they had come to his school, all smiling and asked Mrs Fisher if they could take him from kindergarten – they were going on vacation, Mommy said and then she smiled at Mrs Fisher and added, just for the weekend. Michael didn't know where vacation was but he was hoping you could go fishing there. His Daddy had promised to take him fishing soon, but they hadn't gone yet and it seemed a long time since he'd been waiting.

When he got into the car Michael didn't see a fishing rod but he was surprised and happy anyway because they brought his crayons and a new dot-to-dot book. They were with his clothes and shoes in the back of the sedan. As Daddy drove, Mommy sang. She had a wonderful voice. The song was in the old language she used when she was very happy or very sad. Michael remembered the smells of holidays when she sang: soup with chicken and noodles and sweet wine, which he was only allowed a sip of. His Daddy was humming along.

But they were a long time in the car. It was dark now and there was nothing outside the window that he could see, except for the shadows of the mountains ahead and alongside them. The road was straight and narrow and there were no road signs to practise reading or lights from the streets or gas stations or houses. There was nothing out there at all and Mommy had stopped singing. From the back seat, Michael could tell she was sleeping. Her breathing was heavy and a rhythmic snore was coming from her open mouth. She's even noisy when she sleeps, Daddy said softly. And why you don't lie down across the seat and get some sleep yourself, Daddy said. Michael felt hungry. He wanted to tell Daddy, but didn't. Instead he did as he was told: he stretched out the length of the backseat and tried not to slide around on the shiny leather upholstery, he thought he might be able to hold on with his fingers, so he teased and then pulled at the tiny threads on the seat until he fell asleep.

He woke up on a strange bed. It was strange because it was too big. At home he slept on the small cot in his very own room, his toys around him. This room had two of big beds in it – the one he was in and another one which if he reached out, he could touch. There was a bathroom joining the room and from it he could hear his Mommy singing again and then there was a knock on the door. The door was in the same room as the beds. This scared Michael even more – his bed was next to the front door? He wanted to go home. He was hungry. But when Mommy came through the room and opened the door, it was Daddy carrying a grocery bag and he was with a big lady. The big lady threw her arms around Mommy and kissed her and Mommy screamed out a little and cried in the old language and then they looked at the bed and then the lady almost fell on top of him: hugging him; crying kayn aynhoreh, kayn aynhoreh; yanking him from the warm sheets and then she threw him almost over her shoulder and danced with him, kayn aynhoreh, look how big you are, and kissed him some more. He was wet with her kisses and he began to cry.

'There, there, baby boy.' There was more laughter. Were they laughing at him? He cried some more.

'It's Aunt Charlotte, beautiful boy,' his Mommy said, 'She's happy to see you.'

Then Daddy began to unpack bagels and lox from

the grocery bag and Aunt Charlotte took a toy car from a pocket somewhere within the folds of her dress. It was magic.

Now on the pavement, Michael remembered the car and took it out of his pocket. He held it in his hand and peered in through the store window again. He could see his Daddy there among the men and women gathered around the long table. They were all looking at a man at one end of it. He was rolling dice in his long fingers, blowing on them and letting them slide from his hand across the table. Though the man was very fat, his fingers were long and he teased the dice and the crowd before each throw. Michael could hear the way the crowd was holding its breath and then letting out a cheer of relief or a low moan of disappointment every time. Mostly the crowd was happy though and the man was smiling until his expression changed to serious again as he took the dice back into his long fingers.

Michael could see his Mommy too; she had a drink in her hand now and she was standing closer to Daddy and watching the fat man all the time. She still looked pretty, but also a little bit like when she got mad at him sometimes.

Knowing for certain that he was not being watched back, Michael put his bag of grapes on the pavement and kneeling down began to play with the sleek black Pontiac.

'Vroom, vroom, whatdja think you're doing, you crazy driver?' He'd heard Daddy say this a zillion times at home in the Los Angeles traffic.

Michael revved up the car again and let it go.

'Vroom, crash.' The Pontiac crashed into the wall beneath the store window.

Michael looked up and down the street. There was no one coming. He would see how far and how fast it would go. He glided the car back and forth and back and forth again. Revving her up, Michael let her go with all his might. It must have gone hundreds of miles down the pavement. He had to run quickly to the next doorway to get it back. He ran as fast as he could and back again just in case Daddy came out and looked for him. He didn't want Daddy to take off his belt and strap him.

Back in his place he stood up for a moment and thought about eating the Hershey Bar or his grapes. He put his hand into his pocket and felt that the chocolate had softened and when he pulled his fingers out, he could see that some of the chocolate was on his fingers melted; he was making a mess. He would have to take it out of there and throw it away before his Mommy saw. He would, in a minute, but first he wanted to race the car down the street again. See if he could make it go faster. He peered through the window one more time and saw that the same man was still rolling the dice; the crowd, including his Mommy and Daddy, were still watching the man and the dice, still drinking and talking and laughing with all the other people. Michael bent down and revved the car again. Back and forth and back and forth. Then he let it go, pushing it from him with every ounce of his strength. But within only a few miles its sleek black body was stopped by the crunch of a sleek black boot that came down on top of it in a purposeful stride. The boot did not hesitate in its destruction, but kept on its path in the direction of Michael.

Through quick tears of rage, Michael looked for the face of the person who belonged to the boot. He looked up to the sky and saw two of them. Two bad faces. The first man had black, black hair on his head and on his face. It was neatly cut, but the man's eyes were wild, darting about looking at everything – the traffic on the road, the storefronts, the people he passed, but he didn't look down at Michael and he did not look back to see how he'd crushed the Pontiac, dead. The other man was scary too. He had a rounder face and not so much hair. He was almost running to keep up with the strides of the first bad man. He was puffing and with one hand wiping the sweat from his large face with a handkerchief. The thing that made him really scary was the shiny blade of the big knife he carried in his other hand.

They walked fast and in a few seconds had passed Michael without seeing him. They turned into Aunt Charlotte's doorway. Michael did not take his eyes off them as they marched to where the fat man was rolling the dice with his long fingers, teasing the crowd, laughing. Michael stared through the window and watched as the man who had killed his Pontiac took the knife quickly from his friend and sliced open the fat man's throat.

Through the shrieking and the chaos of people stumbling out the door and onto the street, running in every direction – some of them chasing the bad men, most of them running every other way, Michael couldn't hear his own screaming, 'My car, my car, Daddy!

Thanksgiving

There was the smell of turkey: buttery hot; crackled skin and vaguely garlic. One of the chipped apple dishes was filled with sage and bread crumbs. Coarse onions fought to escape from the stuffing.

Ellie could see her mother's hand holding the apple dish out to her, offering. If she tried hard enough, Ellie might be able to see her mother's face.

But then it was gone – the phone rang. It must be morning. I knew he'd call.

'Hello,' she said, 'Hugh?'

'You knew it was me, Ma. How do you always know?'

'So who else should be calling me at six-thirty in the morning. Where are you?'

'Today I'm in Holland, Ma. It's great, but all business. Not much time to tilt at windmills. I haven't forgotten though. Happy Thanksgiving, Ma. What are your plans for the day?'

'Oh you know – nothing much. Michelle called and asked me to the White House, but who wants to get that dressed up? Ha, don't worry, Hugh, I'm fine.'

She tried to sound fine.

After he hung up, she tried to go back to sleep for awhile. She read or heard somewhere that if she found her sleep position, she might be able to find the dream again. Use up the day. Stay in bed until eleven. See my mother's face.

By seven-thirty, she was out of bed, bathed, powdered, dressed and ready. She sat with her coffee watching Macy's Thanksgiving Day Parade live from New York City. Once, when he was small, Hugh begged them to take him to the parade. He thought it was somewhere close by. She had to explain that New York was on the other side of America. It was a cold place at Thanksgiving. See all the people in their warm coats and hats watching the floats and the balloons and the marching bands. Hugh understood then; rushed out into the sunshine to play on his bicycle with the other children. Every child in the street waiting for their relatives to arrive, the table to be set, the turkey to be carved. Pumpkin pie afterwards. But children hate pumpkin pie, so they are allowed ice cream. Hugh's favorite was Rocky Road – marshmallows and peanuts in ice cream. Outrageous!

Time passed. At ten, the parade was finishing. New Yorkers were eating their dinner. Ellie decided she should cook something for herself. It would be the first time ever alone and she hadn't let herself think ahead or plan for it. But there was a store on the corner run by Armenians. It would be open.

Her neighborhood was quiet, filled with apartment buildings. The sort of people who lived here were the sort of people who went somewhere else for the holidays. There were no kids on the street. For one thing it was a boulevard, a main drag – not safe for kids. Traffic, pollution, dangerous people. You never knew who was about.

The Armenian store was busy. Ellie concentrated on what Thanksgiving dinner should be like. Turkey, stuffing, sugary peas with tiny onions, wild rice. Her mother had made sweet potatoes with brown sugar and melted marshmallows. It was her speciality and when Ellie and Ben began to host Thanksgiving, her mother always brought a dish of yams out to the house. Their house in the Valley was bigger than her parents' apartment in Culver City and they'd had Hugh by then. She could see them now, arriving in the old black Nova, her father driving slowly through the mountain pass between Santa Monica and the Valley. He avoided freeways for his wife's sake; she was frightened by the speed of the other cars.

Ellie's mother would gather the dishes she'd brought with her from the car. Hugh would nearly topple her over in his excitement at their arrival. Her mother would be giving instructions as she entered the house. 'I hope the gas is on low, Eleanor, these yams are still warm. I've bought some peaches and I've got the pie. How big a turkey did you get?'

Ellie's father would be outside for awhile seeing to the car, wiping bugs from the windscreen, talking football scores to Ben.

The store had a spit-oven cooking chickens slowly. Ellie could smell their brown sweetness. The man next to her asked for half – she would have the other half. On the shelves she found a tin of peas and a packet of Stovetop stuffing. Just add water. She asked the daughter of the Armenians if they had any sweet

89

potatoes. The girl did not understand her.

'Yams,' she asked again loudly.

The girl shook her head and went on dusting.

Ellie found the cakes next to the bread shelf. There were three packets left of Sara Lee's individual pumpkin pie. They had some nerve selling such a sliver for $3.10 but she took one anyway.

Back at her apartment, she laid her purchases out on the table. It would only take half an hour to prepare. What to do until it's time to eat? She flicked through a magazine, attempted a crossword. Finally she went into the living room and put on the TV. The first thing was Oprah discussing holiday loneliness so she reached for the remote. *The Wizard of Oz* was showing on KTLA. Dorothy and the Tin Man were singing and dancing on the yellow-brick road on CBS. On channel KCOP, there was a religious service. And 5 was showing a repeat of *The Waltons*.

Ellie sat back in Ben's chair. It was the kind of chair that if you sat right into it, held the arms and pushed in with your back, the leg rest popped out. Soon John-boy's voice was fading and Ellie was asleep again. She dreamt of Ben. He was at a family party with her mother and father. Hugh was not there. Why wasn't Hugh there? Ben was crying because he could not find her. Ellie could see him, but he couldn't see her. And he was crying and so upset. He was not young, nearly 70 and crying as if his heart would break. She was saying: 'Honey, I'm here. I'm over here.' But he couldn't find her, he was pushing her parents around and looking under the furniture for her. He didn't want to lose her. How could he have lost her?

Ellie woke with a start. Her throat was dry and there were tears on her cheeks. She pushed herself back into the chair and closed her eyes. Just to be able to see them again. It all goes so fast.

She tried to eat her dinner. The chicken was a little bit dry. Who knows how long those things go around on that spit? The Stovetop tasted like fake stuffing that you add water to. The worse thing was that she'd forgot Ben's favorite part – the cranberry sauce. She'd forgotten all about it. Now remembering, it was all no good. She threw it all into the garbage disposal. Listened while the sink ate the Thanksgiving dinner.

While the machine crunched chicken bones, Ellie remembered a bottle of whiskey Ben kept in the house for visitors. She found it under the kitchen sink. There was more than half a bottle left. She wondered about the dreaming. Would the whiskey help her back to sleep so that she could dream some more? She took some indigestion tablets to protect her from that terrible food. And some pain killers, just what she had in the house.

When Hugh let himself into Ellie's apartment two days later, he half knew what to expect; he'd been phoning and getting no reply. He thought she looked peaceful reclining in Ben's chair. An old *Quincy* on the TV.

Looking at the Sky

Alan looks towards the sky whenever we walk. We've been married for 18 years and I have accepted that Alan doesn't say much at the best of times, but whenever he suggests a walk across fields or up to the Garth, I usually accept the invitation because there's the chance that he might talk to me. I'd like us to talk about something more important than birds.

But he's often looking up for birds and when he sees something that interests him, he'll say: Look at that buzzard. They're always around here somewhere – two of them. If you see one, his mate is nearby. There it is, look.

It has always been like this. He looks up and around and I look downwards. If either of us were to find a fiver, it would be me.

We don't walk that often now. Our teenagers need to be driven places and between us we have two jobs and two cars, and we're always moving in two different directions. Still I know he is looking up and outwards when he's driving. His car is higher than mine, one of those four-wheel things popular in our neighbourhood. I bet that farmers everywhere make fun of people like him driving huge land-working vehicles to their offices in town. But in his defence he bought it for a good reason: safety, he said. But the reason he *likes* it is that he wants to see over the hedges and be closer to the sky as he drives.

I have learned that when children get to adolescence, one parent or the other becomes personal enemy number one. It's Alan in our house. Because he is overly worried about their safety, because he drives slowly, because he looks at things and takes his time.

These were the things I liked about him when I first met him. His carefulness and his patience meant he not only got things done, he got them done well. I was slapdash and quick. But now I find that I often see Alan through the eyes of our children and that I'm more impatient than ever. I don't find nearly enough fivers as we need to pay for everything.

'New trainers are how much?' I seem to ask this kind of question every Saturday morning.

'About sixty-five pounds for the ones I need,' says Jake, our fourteen year old. His sister sniggers in her older, wiser way.

'The ones you need –' she says, 'bullshit.'

'Laura,' Alan says it quietly, but quickly, 'there's no need to swear.'

She rolls her eyes at him. He doesn't see. I see. And I see that he is never going to stop them from swearing. Never. Unless they want to stop themselves. Just like being an alcoholic or a bulimic. You gotta want to stop.

She pushes her messy plate of half eaten toast away. Half eaten? I mean, a bit of the middle eaten.

For Laura, the dimensions of what constitutes the crust of the bread – the bit you are allowed to leave until you are a grown up – has escalated out of proportion to its whole.

'Well, she's right,' I say, 'I can get trainers, which by the way, last me a year or more, for less than 30 pounds.'

I know it would be better to back Alan up about the swearing just at that point. I know she needs, more than anything else, some kind of joint discipline from us. But openly I don't care about the words she chooses to express herself with. I know that she is getting ready to get up and leave the table and I want to keep her there as long as I can.

'See,' she says and she makes the face at Alan. The face consists of more eye rolling accompanied by a kind of tongue gymnastics, which distorts the mouth and nose into something terrifying. I don't know why she does it: it makes her look so awful. Still it has become a part of our everyday lives, particularly at mealtimes.

I wish I could be like Alan. He never sees it. And he doesn't notice that she leaves the table anyway – and that she heads directly for the toilet upstairs.

'What about the shoes?' Jake says to me. He doesn't make faces at Alan yet; he just addresses all his questions to me.

'Okay,' I say. It's just easier.

When did I become the stronger parent? The one they come to with everything. The one who sees everything? I know things that I don't want to know.

Why can't I be more like Alan? If you analyse it, he should be the one they go to. The steady one, the one with morals and manners and codes to live by. The one with the strong family background. The one of us who owns a Bible and occasionally reads it.

There was a time when we were happy. I remember when we lived near the Thames and we used to walk just down from Walton Bridge. Once when Jake was really little, too little to notice the houseboats moored across on the Shepperton side or the young men we passed who were wearing no shirts, playing with a Frisbee, celebrating the god of summer, he was in his push chair and became so fascinated by his own bare toes and I watched him reaching for them, capturing them, eating the biggest one. I laughed then and shouted to Alan. He was nearer to the edge of the river, kneeling and holding Laura with his arm tight around her waist. She was open handed, offering bread to a swan that was bigger than she was. She had no fear. The two of them looked up and towards Jake and me at the same time. Alan and Laura; the same concentrated forehead, the same slow smile. I remember that moment's happiness.

Lately, I am, more than anything else, a grown up. Smart and sensible enough to know that these things will pass. The concerns of now will become other worries later. I even know that in the whole scheme of things, some of this stuff – the face making and the eye rolling particularly – isn't really that important. My days are punctuated by news bulletins and special reports and I know about what's happening out in the world. We are lucky to be living here on this still gentle, rural border. We could be bringing up our children in Zimbabwe or Afghanistan or Iraq. We could be sending them out for new shoes to the markets and stores of Jerusalem or Islamabad or Karachi in the conviction that we need to show the world how we carry on with our lives despite the fear one of us or all of us might be caught up in something bad, impossible, fatal. Something that would separate us forever. This is how I justify giving Jake eighty quid to spend on trainers and the bus fare into Cardiff and to have some lunch at McDonald's.

Eighty quid. It makes him happy. I think it even makes me happy for a moment.

When he leaves, he shouts bye Mum from the front door and slams it hard behind him. Alan is out in the back garden, starting up the lawn mower. I bring him some coffee and it's noticeable that he doesn't ask me about the money for Jake, or how he's going to get into town or what time he will be back.

I say, 'Laura will want a lift to work later. I have some shopping to do and laundry.'

He says, 'I'll take her. What time does she start?'

He's not looking at me so I roll *my* eyes. She has been working at the leisure centre for nearly a year of Saturday afternoons and she has always started at one.

Why do I find this so hard?

Why do other people do domesticity with such apparent ease?

It is all my fault?

Eight years have passed since. It is hard to believe. Jake had only started school and Laura was still a little girl learning to skip rope, learning to read, do sums. Looking back, I remember a lot of grey, but that was just their school uniforms.

I see myself ironing them on a Sunday evening and planning it all out.

If I am organised about getting the kids to school just a little bit earlier than strictly acceptable, I could come back to the house and have time to get ready. Very ready. Shave my legs and farther up. Make-up. Hair. By the time I was finished with my hair, it wouldn't be too early to have a small drink for courage. Wine, if there was any left over from the night before, or if not, there was always a little whisky in the house. But not too much to drink, everything had to be perfect. It may have been *his* uniform. Or was I just so immature and in need of attention? He was our second delivery postman. I had never seen anybody look so good when they smiled. I still don't know when or why it became so important to catch his eye every day, to meet him at the door by accident, on purpose. It didn't take long for him to realise what I was up to. And then all those long coffee breaks, first just inside the porch, then in my kitchen. One day, he only asked to use the loo and I took it as my right as the housewife – wife of the house – to lead him up the stairs, show him the way.

That was before we moved here and I grew up. Before we had two cars. Before the children were old enough to judge me, thank god. Alan never judged me, even when I confessed to him after six months and four and a half gin and tonics. He thought it out quietly for exactly three days and then waited for me to come out of the bathroom after my shower. I had a big white towel wrapped around me. He was sitting on the top stair.

He said, 'I want to keep our family together. Is that what you want?'

Just then I didn't think I had any right to want anything, but I said I wanted the same thing.

We moved to a new house in a different place and I went back to work. We got a new bed and bedroom furniture and I really thought that we could start again. Later, the kids went on to comprehensive school and got smarter and smarter in so many ways.

Today, Alan says, 'Shall we take a walk?'

The lawn is mowed. The shopping is put away. Laura is at work. Jake is in town. Why not?

Instead of heading towards the river as I thought we might, Alan strides towards the woods. Our walks are as silent as our lives when the children aren't around. I wonder if he is as frustrated with this as I am. I long to talk to him about the news or about the unhealthy amount of money I have given Jake today or tell him of my fears for Laura. I long to say I'm sorry.

He is looking at the sky. There is a frown on his face. He looks deeply worried. Not for the first time, I notice how he is ageing. Deep lines surround his eyes; age spots his hands. His eyes themselves, they seem to be duller. Did I do this to him when I ruined our easy happiness? Did I do this to all of us for a few hours in bed with the second delivery postman?

And then the familiar inner voice; I physically ache at its nagging anticipation: *This is it. He has brought me out here to tell me that it's not getting any better. You can't just move house and then wait and hope: there are some things you never get over.*

This is my fear; the thing I always expect him to say. For eight years, I've been making myself ready for this moment. Now I almost will him to say it finally.

But I forget how smart Alan is; how this is my punishment. Alan is quiet and Alan will make me wait forever before he speaks of it.

'You see it,' he says pointing upwards.

'Yes, I see. It's the buzzard, right?'

'It's been alone for days. I keep spotting it flying low; looking at something in these woods.'

He walks even faster. He looks up frequently keeping the lonely buzzard in his sight.

We walk like that for half a mile or so and then I see it. The dead-for-days carcass of a large bird – the buzzard's mate. I knew that I would be the one to see it first – the way I'm always the one of us looking down.

Alan makes a move toward it and without thinking I reach for his arm so that I can hold him back with me, protect him. I'm surprised when he lets himself be stopped. I'm surprised when he takes his other hand and covers mine with it. I'm surprised that we stand together like that for a long time.

The Reunion

Scan and email proofs to P for approval. Pick up dry cleaning (maybe not today). Studio: start commission from C (still buzzing she likes the idea!!) Quick ham sandwich (but nothing else and remember mayo is forbidden!!!). More work (get something done!) Telephone Harry. Telephone Bernie? Shower. Hair (use hot oil shampoo). Shave legs.

I chewed on my pen reading the list over. Thinking about how much time it would take to get ready, what to wear. I looked at the biro; all its bite marks – no idea where it came from in the first place and, yet, here I was eating it instead of breakfast.

'Uck,' I said, breaking the quiet, 'you're disgusting.'

Make yourself look fabulous (or as fabulous as possible), I added to the bottom of the list.

I got up from the desk, crossed the room. The office – my office was a desk in the corner of the bedroom – my bedroom. I sat on the bed – on my side of the bed, remembering again that it was all my side now. Then I looked into the full-length mirror. Okay. Not glamorous, but not too shabby either. Hair – mostly the color it had been, though there had been other colors through the years. Now it was back to dark blonde or mousy, depending on who was describing it – someone nice to me, or me. My face had perhaps filled out a bit in twenty years, but that was not a bad thing. So skinny in high school. Short and bony – a tomboy. Always in the trees with Harry. Then on the girls' baseball and track teams. A whole generation before it was sexy for girls to play first baseman and run. Nerdy in those days. Something you did because you couldn't make the cheerleading squad. Kay was a cheerleader. Kay had been beautiful; shiny real blonde hair, long legs. She curved in all the right places. The boys all liked her, but Kay wouldn't go out with any of them. Just wanted to be with me. Beautiful Kay Sullivan wanted to be with quiet Edith Fazekas, who had skinny legs and no boobs. Well at least now I have boobs that I could show them. That last thought made me giggle.

That's all you have to do, Edith. Turn up alone at the Sheridan Universal Hotel to party with my old classmates from high school for the first time in twenty years and say hi there, remember me? You don't? That's because I've got breasts now. See!!!

That would cause a stir. Just before graduation they voted me Class Pancake and Most Likely NOT To Be Spotted In A Porno Flick. Something to take with you and remember forever. Kay had been voted Sexiest Laugh.

I tried to push thoughts of Kay to the back of my mind, never an easy task. It was even more natural to think of her on a day such as this. Thinking of high school. Thinking of what came after. I suppose by now most people will know, but what if someone missed all that commotion and asks, so where's Kay? You were always together. I'd just assumed you'd still know each other.

And they'd be right, of course, because we probably would have gone to the reunion together. With similar-looking husbands and matching dresses.

I shouldn't even be going. It's supposed to be a happy occasion. Just tell the truth, but the truth itself was blurry. Was it an accident or...? That's what the police thought and what they'd said to Kay's parents. Accidental. Like our friendship.

Kay and Edith, the most unlikely of best friends.

Tenth grade. First week of high school. My mother always bought me a new dress for the first day of school. Problem was, that year it was long-sleeved and woollen – suitable for winter in Connecticut maybe, but not sweltering September in southern California. The other girls went back to school in shorts and t-shirts, thongs or sandals on their bare feet. But my mother disapproved. California was a new place to her, even then, with its culture based on year-round sunshine. I can hear the way she used to complain regularly and bitterly about the heat and lack of real weather. She missed the seasons changing. She missed her family back east.

Yet when it came to September, usually the hottest month of all, and 'Back to School' (advertised loudly by all the big department stores), my mother forgot the heat and concentrated on the impression. Her daughter was to dress decently, respectfully with proper shoes and socks. She chose pleated skirts, frilly blouses and wool dresses and expected me to wear them.

(It was only later when Kay showed me the trick of bringing shorts and thongs to school in my PE bag and changing in the girls' bathroom first thing that I started to look like the other girls.)

But that first day, I was wearing the dress. It was gray. Fitted tight. Which made it worse considering my shape. You could be useful in woodwork, we're always looking for a flat surface, the boys taunted more than once. Of course in those days no girl ever entered a workshop, just as the boys weren't allowed in Home Ec. – what we called, cooking and sewing.

I sat in the front row in biology, the first one there, punctual just like I'd been in junior high. (That too would change with Kay.) The classroom started to fill up and then just as the teacher, Mr Waterhouse (he spoke with a broad Boston accent and was in the habit of inviting the seniors to 'staa paatiees' at his house, where they could view the constellations through his super strength telescope), was about to close the door Kay came in with six or seven of her friends.

They were so cool. Their halter tops showed off tanned skin, their hot pants revealed smooth legs. Yet even amongst them Kay stood out – the best looking, the best dressed, the most confident. Always noticed first.

She pointed at me. Look there's seats here together, she said.

She had a half smile on her face and even Mr Waterhouse stopped what he was saying as she commanded her friends to sit down. But when they all sat, the row was one seat short, leaving Kay standing.

Her smile faded, her look directed at me, and I started to gather my books, to stand and to move towards the back of the class.

'Sit down,' Mr Waterhouse said to me so forcefully that I dropped my things onto the floor. To Kay, he said, 'There's a seat for you at the back.' To the class he said, 'Can we make a staat now?'

Kay moved to the back, and I, trying to collect my things from the floor, wanting to disappear, did not see the look of anger and then pity that I imagined Kay fixed me with. Taking in the gray dress, the flat chest. Taking it all in.

Thinking of Kay never did any good. I tried to concentrate on my list. The things I needed to do. But in the studio, really a spare bedroom with a drafting table and a computer, I could only manage the automatic jobs − sharpening my favourite pencils, laying out photographs all over the beige carpet. The easy things. I was thinking so hard that it seemed as if Kay was with me. Being with her again was an uncomfortable place, but I couldn't help it.

It's funny the things you remember from high school. Like how Kay arranged our senior prom dates with James and Jeffrey Watanabe (voted Most Studious X 2) four months before the tickets even went on sale. Kay didn't actually want to be with them, but, in those days, dates were required. And we had to go together, it was a rule. So how better than with the twins? Both so quiet, so scared of girls that they couldn't believe their luck. (A cheerleader, after all, was a big deal and Kay the biggest deal of all.) She planned it: one car, one set of before photos. One hotel room afterwards. Lots of Boone's Farm sweet strawberry wine, which the boys were to get somehow. No kissing, no touching. Those were the rules. James and Jeffrey wouldn't dare to make a move anyway, that's one of the reasons they were chosen. I never even knew which one of them was supposed to be my date. As it happened they faithfully took us to the Holiday Inn afterwards, had one drink and left. Kay and I so wrapped up in each other, our new dresses, didn't even see them go.

Just before the big night, another boy asked me to go with him. I think I liked him too. Felt flattered, was tempted. What was his name?

Another memory. The time that I went along with Kay and the other song queens and raided the boys' locker room during the varsity homecoming game. We only stole the clean towels, oh and the coach's spare jock strap, which Kay removed from his desk drawer with a Baggie taped on her hand, so that she wouldn't have to touch it. (Later that week, someone – who? – hung it from the flagpole in the quadrant.)

Then there was the time we drank the contents of Kay's parents' cocktail cabinet. Just the two of us alone in the big ranch-style house for the night. I was sick in the hot tub Kay's family kept in the garden. When Kay's parents, eventually, complained that all their liquor had disappeared, Kay made them believe that she was suffering from some teenage emotional crisis and they forgave her generously. It never would have been so easy at my house, with my parents. And just for coming home in one of Kay's oversized bikini tops the next day, I was grounded for a week. Kay found that part of it hilarious, of course.

Back further to the beginning. Those first weeks of high school. After that encounter in biology, I tried to stay out of Kay's way. Ate a packed lunch with Harry in the yard. Didn't even bother with the cafeteria. Harry wanted me to join the Spanish Club with him and Knights and Ladies (if I could keep up a 3.5 grade-point-average) and the Chess Club. He used to bring his portable chess set to school and show me his best moves at lunchtime.

But it was hard not to notice Kay. Always in trouble. Running down the corridor, banging lockers, hurling herself off the bleachers. We thought she was a show-off. And always behind her there was some teacher or Mrs Howard, the vice-principal, saying Kay Sullivan, stop running shouting jumping. Or Miss Sullivan get to class.

But in class, she was just as bad. (And she was in all of my classes.) The problem was (and if I could see it, why couldn't the teachers?) that she was smart. She found the work too easy and that's why she couldn't stop talking, whispering, laughing, writing notes, throwing things across the room at one of her pep squad friends.

The only way to keep Kay quiet, one or two of the teachers found, was to make her sit with someone quiet, someone unpopular, someone studious and too afraid to chat and pass notes when a teacher was talking. Someone so boring that she wouldn't bother with them.

They made her sit with me.

One after the other. It was as if it was decided in the staff room. Or at a meeting of the faculty. Or as if Mr Waterhouse told Miss Feilich and Miss Feilich told Mrs Syde. If you want to control Kay Sullivan, make her sit with Edith Fazekas.

First Kay raged, she stormed, she sulked. But then she changed, no not into someone like me, no way. What she did was simple and smart. I always knew she was smart. She changed me into someone like her. It was subtle. At first, she was just nice. Then she was fun and generous. She told me how she smuggled clothes and makeup from her house and came into school early to get ready. She invited me to the Friday night football games with her crowd and to the pizza place afterwards. She taught me to smoke, before she decided that it was stupid and we would not do it anymore.

We were friends before I knew it. I just forgot Harry. Never joined the Chess Club or bothered with the Ladies. I did make the track team, but that was only because some PE teacher or other told me I should try out. It was about the same time that Kay went out for the cheerleading squad. And Kay said, yeah go for it. It could be fun.

And then one day Kay said something that clarified our friendship. We were dissecting a cow's eyeball in Mr Waterhouse's class. Kay did the cutting and separating and I drew the diagrams for the worksheet.

I felt sick. There were remnants of blood and sticky pus in the bowl with the eye. I did our drawing with one hand holding my forehead trying not to look, my stomach turning.

'I couldn't have done that,' I said watching Kay lift the lens from behind the cow's slippery gray iris.

'Best friends help each other,' said Kay. She was smiling at my discomfort, but then she added, 'And they do every thing together.'

And I, so grateful, agreed.

***

At three o'clock, I left the studio; it had been a waste of time anyway. I tried to close the door on my thoughts. If I kept this up, I'd be exhausted by the evening. I phoned Harry (Hardest Worker and Biggest Feet). He was a lawyer now, with his own small practice and this would be a good time to get him. Back from lunch. I knew he usually scheduled his clients' meetings in the mornings. No court on the day of the reunion, he'd told me.

He answered his own phone, 'Harry Sixthsmith.'

'Oh. No secretary?'

'Edith, hi. Hello. No she's left for the day. Friday and all that. I told her to go and pick up her kids from school.'

'What a good boss,' I said. 'What about tonight?'

'Tonight is going to be great. So don't worry.' He knew what I was thinking. It came as no surprise; Harry has always known me better than anyone.

'Rog and I will get there nice and early. I promise.

Definitely before you.'

I groaned. The thought of walking in alone. I'd been hoping...

'What?' Harry said.

'I wished you lived nearer. How about if I drive over to you? We could...'

'Yeah that's smart, you drive all the way over here so that the three of us can drive all the way up to Universal City together and that should add at least another hour to your travelling time. Maybe two as you'll be hitting the 405 at rush hour. Very clever. Look, you'll be fine. All you have to do is...'

'Walk in alone. The only woman with no man, I bet.'

For the thousandth time, I wished that Harry was a girl. He's my closest friend – my oldest friend, but he doesn't always get it. A girlfriend would understand. A girlfriend on the other end of the same conversation would say, you can't go to a high school reunion without a date. Especially after what happened with Kay. A girlfriend would say, you can't walk in alone; you'll be scrutinized. Are you crazy? Someone will ask you to explain. And they'll think you're worthless; not even in a relationship. What sort of person are you, they'll want to know. A girlfriend would say stay home and draw pictures of peaches or something, read a book, do anything except go to that reunion on your own.

But there were no girl friends.

There were no other friendships.

After high school, there was college, then jobs. And Kay and I did it all together. I followed her, I know.

Whatever she said, whatever she decided. It was easiest and we both got what we wanted. Until I blew it.

Oh sure, there were acquaintances, contacts. But there were no other friends. So now there was only Harry.

'You've got to do this, Ed. This is the first time you get the chance to show what a strong, independent woman you've become,' he was saying.

Somehow, I managed to stay in touch with Harry all those years. Well, there was a strong bond – we grew up together in the same street. Our mothers live there still. Best friends, even now, shaking their heads over our wasted opportunities while sipping pink gin on each other's patios. They always had this grand plan (which was only half of the joke they make it out to be) that Harry and I would have a massive wedding after college, produce six kids and live happily ever after, preferably on the same street where we grew up. Of course, Harry wasn't interested in girls. I'd always known that, though our mothers took a little longer to realize.

He'd never approved of Kay. From the beginning he pointed out, in his much too mature way, that Kay wanted total possession of me.

And I ignored him. Worse, there was a time when Kay and I launched a major attack on Harry. For years we made fun of him, laughed at him, left him out. He had pimples, couldn't throw a ball and made straight As (except in PE).

He'd forgiven me. After Kay. I didn't deserve it, but as soon as he heard, he was there by my side, supporting me through everything. He let me talk, cry or be silent. He never mentioned the other stuff and how much I must have hurt him when we were kids.

It took a long time. I mourned Kay, sure I did. But also those wasted years. You get this idea that high school is supposed to be the best time of your life. But there's just too much pressure for some. Must be popular; play football; be a cheerleader. But what about those who never fit it? Like Harry. Like me.

Like Kay?

'Oh god,' I said to Harry, 'it was definitely bad timing to split up with Bernie now.'

'You did the right thing and you'll be okay. I promise.'

'That's easy for you to say,' I said, 'you can walk in with Roger and...'

'And some would say that won't be easy either.'

'You'll be fine,' I said and then the whole conversation turned around so that by the time I hung up the phone, it had all turned around. I reassured Harry. I soothed Harry. After all Harry had turned from a spotty nerd into a fabulous-looking, successful attorney. What did he have to worry about? Being gay? Pfft. Half, no, three-quarters of the best people in LA are gay. So I promised Harry that he would have it all: the moon, the sun, the stars and the respect of his fellow graduating class. All he had to do was show up and walk in proudly, with the gorgeous Roger, of course.

I had all the answers. For Harry.

The worst of it was that I had to make another call.

111

I couldn't put it off any longer. I'd promised to speak to Bernie. I promised to give him an answer today. Another answer I didn't have.

You know how they say that men choose the same kind of woman over and over. It's kind of like that for me. Only different, because...well, because I never did the choosing. Except once. Only once did I decide anything and that decision went about as wrong as anything can ever go.

For years I followed Kay, then after Kay I followed Bernie. My husband.

Bernie is an action man. He has this great job. Runs outdoor pursuit vacations for stressed-out business people or for big companies or for whoever will pay him. So he travels a lot. And he gets to scuba dive, jump out of airplanes (with a parachute on, most of the time), climb mountains. When he has spare time, he spends it looking for something exciting to do. So you can imagine what being married to someone like Bernie is like, especially if you are someone like me.

At one time I was happy to hear about his adventures. It was exciting being married to a man who always had a story to tell. I was proud to be with someone who could captivate a crowd.

But, let's face it, I was excluded and mostly, ignored. It took me a while to see it clearly. In fact, I'm still realizing a lot about myself. And our marriage, such as it is, just isn't enough anymore.

No more, that's what I told Bernie last time he was home.

He didn't argue so I thought he agreed. He went on

one of his long trips, which gave me more time to be certain that this was what I wanted. But back in LA, Bernie rented a studio apartment – something far less than permanent. No place to store his stuff. And he started to cajole me, to sweet-talk me. He started to date me and to woo me. He was charming. He was attentive. He wanted to come back.

'We'll sit in the sun together on weekends,' he promised.

'We'll take up golf or read poetry, whatever you want,' he said.

'We'll have a baby.'

How could I believe him?

And now he was waiting for an answer.

I wandered around the house, putting the moment off as long as I could. Fluffed up the pillows on my couch, attacked a cobweb with a broom, tried my voice out. Keep it soft, I told myself, but firm. Mustn't weaken. My voice could give me away. He knows me so well. He will hear lonely, he will hear scared.

Because I was. Lonely, scared and worried. Always, but especially about tonight. Especially about the reunion. Everyone there will be coupled, they will be showing photos of their beautiful kids, I thought. I shouldn't go. It will be depressing – a setback. I should telephone Harry again. He'll understand if I don't make it.

I was only trying to put off talking to Bernie, of course.

But it didn't work. Because before I could decide who I should call, Bernie phoned me.

'Hi honey,' he said. 'What do you think?'

'I wasn't thinking at all. You caught me off guard,' my voice was thin. He would hear angry.

'Bad timing? I'll come over. We can talk things over better if we are face to face.' Nothing deterred him.

'No I, I'm going out. I've got to get ready.'

'Where are you...oh it's that reunion thing, right. I'll come with you, you don't want to walk in alone, do you?'

'No Bernie, listen...'

'Don't worry, I'll go with you.'

'No I. Really, I can't let you. It's something I'd like to do alone.'

He wasn't fooled. He played the ace card.

'You know they'll ask, don't you? They'll want to know all the little details. It's human nature. It'll be like going back in time. If I'm with you...'

'I know that. But I've got to face it. It's time to put it behind me.' Now he would hear lonely. Now he would hear scared. I couldn't help it.

I stopped. Took a breath. Tried again. 'There are people I'd like to see, you know. Friends from a long time ago.'

'Okay, honey, you know what's best for you. I'll be here if you need me.'

I didn't notice how easily he gave it up.

The Sheraton Universal Hotel stands on top of the highest peak in the Hollywood Hills. From its privileged position it looks over both the city of Los Angeles to the south and the San Fernando Valley to the north.

If the hotel could report what it sees, it would say

what everyone else says: Los Angeles is a sprawling metropolis with no center. At night the length and depth of LA can be traced by the snakes, patterns and tracks of streets, highways and freeways that run through it like veins on an addict.

Sunset Boulevard is lit up and moving from Beverley Hills, shopping, banking, palatial residences down through Hollywood's cheap outlet shops and the pimps selling their girls (most of them came here to be 'discovered') in the forecourt of Taco Bell. Then the street winds through Century City and into Santa Monica and finally to the edge of the Pacific where it has no choice but to stop short. On a good night it would take an hour and a half to drive from one end of Sunset to the other.

The hotel's other view is of suburban San Fernando Valley. The place where I grew up. And Kay. The place where we met, went to school, went to college. The place we brought Kay home to. The place we buried her.

But death is not usually associated with the Valley – swimming pools are. Once there were only orange groves and Mexican migrant workers and not much else. Then the trees gave way to hundreds of housing tracks. My parents bought their first (and only) house on one of those developments. Kay's parents did too, though they were both Angelenos. Harry's parents were from the North near the Oregon border. The point is that everyone came here at the same time – and, to them, it seemed like the beginning of something.

Each house was built on enough land to ensure

yards, both at the front and the back. The architects, probably feeling the overwhelming heat in the days before anyone had refrigerated air-conditioning, added a swimming pool to the backyard of one in every five of the houses.

Later, as the suburbanites who came to live in the Valley became more and more affluent, more pools were added. Now we're known as the Swimming Pool Capital of the World. Really. When an incoming plane starts its descent at LAX, the passengers who haven't been there before (and some of the ones who have) gaze down in wonder on the multitude of blue dots.

The American suburban dream.

I decided to avoid the congestion on the 405 interchange and drove through Topanga Canyon into the Valley to catch the 101 which took me straight through the west side of the Valley: Woodland Hills; Encino; Sherman Oaks, Van Nuys, and finally onto the 5 and into Studio City. Then I ascended that great man-made, Hollywood mountain. At the top, I drove into the Universal Studios parking lot and noticed the tourists slowly leaving the theme park. Full of the day they'd spent with King Kong and poking around the Psycho House and in Lucille Ball's dressing room.

I parked as close to the hotel as I could. Checked my face in the rear-view mirror. Took more deep breaths and left the safety of the car. Made my way to the hotel's entrance.

'The first step into the danger zone,' I whispered to myself and then I laughed out loud. Nervous.

What the hell was I doing here?

Walking in alone. The foyer first. Looking for the invitation. It must be here somewhere, fumbling around for it in the bottom of my bag.

'Can I help you madam.'

'I'm looking for the Harrison High School reunion,' I said. My head was more in my bag than out of it.

'There it is,' I said to myself, mostly. I'd found the embossed card. I read it. It said Skywalker Ballroom.

'The Skywalker Ballroom,' the concierge said, ' – through the double doors and on your left, Madam.'

This can't be the right room, I thought, I don't recognise anyone. Wait. Isn't that Wendy Primo? It is.

'Hello,' she said, 'Edith , isn't it? You look great.'

Wendy looked great. Still the same. Confident. (Voted Class Slut – no that can't be right – maybe Perfect Person To Be On A Welcoming Committee.)

She was pinning something on to my dress. A badge with my dreadful senior picture and my name underneath it.

'Is it still Fazekas?' Wendy said.

'It's Davis. Different isn't it? As different as you can get. I couldn't be a Fazeka forever. All that spelling over and over... And no one can say it, I was always called Edith Faeces...'

Oh god, I was prattling on. Did Wendy even hear what I just said? She was smiling at me, but her eyes were on the people coming in behind me. Waiting for me to stop talking so that she could welcome the next guests.

'Nice to see you,' I said and moved farther into the room.

I looked around. No Harry. Not that I could see,

anyway. The room was huge; round tables for ten surrounded the dance floor in the middle. Each of the tables had a centerpiece of luminous balloons. Silver and light blue. I remembered then, our class colors.

Along the back wall was a stage; the band on it was getting ready to play. In front of them a very large DJ was playing records from the 80s. What else? Even from so far away I could see the DJ, because she was wearing the most outrageous outfit, which seemed to sparkle as she moved and danced to the music. An over-the-top Donna Summer look-a-like. She was trying to get someone to dance, trying to shake things up a bit. When the music stopped she was making funny comments, remembering news items from 1987 too, but no one was paying attention. Everyone too busy spotting each other and playing the reunion game.

960 of us graduated that year. 960 people! But looking around, there was no one here familiar to me. Not one familiar face. Someone came over. A man. He was bald. No one in high school had been bald.

'Hi...' he was looking at my chest. Like the weird fantasy, only he was really just looking at my name tag. '...Edith Fa...a...Zee...uh, Edith. Don Mills. Are you alone?'

'Don, hi. Don – did we know each other? I don't remember. Actually I'm supposed to meet Harry Sixthsmith, have you seen him? Did you know him?' I sounded so stupid.

'Sure,' said Don, 'I remember Harry. Biggest Feet, wasn't it? I'll tell you what, I'll get you a drink. White wine, is it? All the ladies drink white wine. Doesn't put weight on, does it.' For some reason, he patted his own tummy and went off.

Nothing else to do, I looked around. More people had arrived. Groups were forming. I wondered if these people kept up with each other, or if it really was the first time they'd met in years. There was laughter and shouting. Recognition. Catching up. All very happy and secure. Just like in school, I felt outside of it. Harry told me that everyone feels the same. Everyone sure was good at hiding it, then and now. Wish I could. Wish I could just go up to one of these groups and say hi, remember me. And someone else would say sure, yes. Good to see you. Remember the time we... Harry said he'd be here. This was even more awful than I thought it was going to be. I wondered if I could sneak out past Wendy Primo.

'Hi Edith. How are you?' It was Terri Morris. (Most likely to Succeed, Best Teeth.) She'd been a cheerleader with Kay. One of the gang. She was, maybe, a bit chubbier now. Her hair was short and stylishly cut. It had been long, really long, and tied back.

'I haven't seen you for ages,' she said.

Since the funeral, I thought.

Then she hugged me. It was a sort of false, quick hug, but I felt myself returning the squeeze, even holding on a second too long.

'I'll always remember the time you chucked a Coke over Neil Trotter's head,' Terri said.

What?

'What?' I said.

'He sure was cute. He was on the football team,

remember? You must remember him; he made the All-Americans in 11th grade. That's him over there with his wife,' she pointed towards the bar at a middle-aged man, gray moustache and beard, not much hair. Attractive woman next to him.

I took a breath. 'That...um...that must have been Kay.'

At the mention of Kay's name, Terri paused. Was she thinking: why weren't you there with her, you were her friend, couldn't you have saved her? Is that what Terri would say next? And then I would say...what? What would I say?

It wasn't my fault. It wasn't my fault. It wasn't my fault. Breathe. Breathe.

'You really don't remember Neil? Terri asked as if this was a major problem. 'He followed you around for two whole semesters.'

'That must have been Kay, too.' I tried again. Maybe if I kept mentioning her name...

'What was?'

'It was Kay he was following around.'

'Really. I always thought it was you. Oh well, there you go. I hated you for no reason then,' she said and she slapped my arm playfully.

'I can't remember him,' I said, as if I was apologizing.

This was a very strange conversation. Not the one I'd expected to have. At least my breathing was back to normal though.

'...he's a dentist, too.' Terri was saying.

'Neil Trotter? That's great,' I said.

'No. Not Neil — my fiancé. I met him at a

conference. I thought I wanted a career, but it looks like I'm going to try the housewifey thing. It's actually not that exciting looking in people's mouths all day.'

What else was there to say? I kept smiling and nodding, and feeling like I'd missed something.

'Look it's great to see you,' Terri finally said, 'but I think I should get back to my fiancé. Are you alone? You can come and sit with us if you like.'

'I'm meeting Harry. Harry Sixthsmith, but thanks.'

Terri looked relieved. She walked back towards her fiancé. He was with a group of people who seemed to know each other well. The fiancé was older. Maybe much older. Looked nice though. He smiled wide at Terri when he saw her coming towards him. Opened his arm for her to come into. They fitted each other, his arm around her back. They even laughed in unison when Terri saw someone else she recognised, introduced the new arrival to him. Shared a memory. It must have been something really, really funny.

Then I saw Don Mills. He was coming back, carrying drinks. Looking for me. A huge grin on his face. What in the world would we say to each other? Where was Harry? I should have brought Bernie. I'm no good without Bernie, I thought. And then, by some miracle, Don Mills, was intercepted by someone else saying hey Don Mills do you remember me?

I moved quickly. Made my way to the other side of the ballroom. Looking for a bathroom. Or the kitchen. Looking for somewhere to hide. Not just from Don. From the whole nightmare.

I must have looked like something, striding aggressively through the commotion of people remembering each other and tables, over the dance floor and past the stage – the shiny DJ still dancing around, but I don't think anyone looked or noticed or stared. They kept right on re-uniting and rediscovering. I didn't know where I was going or what I was going to do once I got there.

Almost on cue, a door opened as I approached and three men dressed in white suits like John Travolta in *Saturday Night Fever* entered the ballroom and made their way to the stage – the entertainment.

Wrong decade, I thought as they passed me and then, without thinking anything else, I took their place in the room they'd just exited, closing the door behind me.

The dressing room I found myself in wasn't much bigger than a closet. There were a couple of chairs, a clothes rack with a few items still hanging on it, a mirror, not much else. I could smell hairspray and deodorant, cold strong coffee. I dropped onto one of the chairs, leaned my head backwards against the wall and closed my eyes.

I should have been thinking of a way to leave gracefully and I should've been angry at Harry.

But I was thinking of Kay.

Kay would have loved all this. She was great at parties. Had a real talent for getting noticed and making herself the center of attraction. And yet, she kept everyone who wanted to know her better (and everyone did want to know her better) at arm's length. A party was Kay's perfect venue.

I'd never ever been the attraction, but when I was at a party with Kay, I wasn't far from the center.

Even her funeral was a big affair. And sad. Of course. So sad.

But.

Only twenty-three, the minister had said. Nothing but the sad waste of a young, beautiful, talented girl with so much to live for. But he didn't know her, so everything he said felt impersonal. Of course, it was sad; of course it was a waste; of course she was beautiful. But what about Kay? I remember looking at her mom and dad and all those shocked people. I was thinking, does anyone else know who we're talking about? Kay was more than pretty, she was more than popular.

No one at the funeral asked what was she like? What was she really like? Or how could this have happened? And there was no one to blame. Just dumb acceptance. A young girl, drunk, walks in front of a bus. Was I the only one who found this hard to believe?

And now, tonight, there was nothing. It was as if Kay had never been in high school with the rest of us. And if she was never there, then what am I doing here? Because Kay was all I knew of high school. And the only way I was known.

Oh god. How do I get out of here?

The door opened and I could hear the singers. They were making a mess of *Heart of Glass*. It was barely recognisable. Underneath the tinny sound, I could still hear hundreds of people talking and laughing. Then the door closed, the music and the laughter faded again and I heard breathing, smelled thick perfume. I opened my eyes. The DJ was in the dressing room with me. She was blue-sequinned from her toes to her neck.

She didn't hesitate when she saw me; she sat on the other chair. It was only a little chair and I don't know where she put herself, but she did it gracefully.

From somewhere she produced a packet of Virginia Slims. Offered me one.

'I don't,' I said.

'You won't mind if I do?' she said.

How could I mind? I was in her space, not the other way around.

'You won't tell nobody, will you, Sugar?'

'Absolutely not,' I said.

She took a long drag on her smoke. It was something she really needed. Then she said, 'You look all done in. Aren't you having a wonderful time?'

'Oh sure,' I said, 'Great. I don't know anyone. I'm alone…'

'Oh,' she said, 'you're a wife. I've done this gig hundreds of times and I can always tell the wives; bored, lonely, not overwhelmed to meet hubby's first sweetheart. It won't be long now, doll.'

'No,' I said. 'Not a wife.'

'Oh,' she said. She looked at her cigarette for a minute, then she looked at me again. Trying to think of something to say.

I have this effect on everyone I meet.

So we sat there in silence. Her smoking and me thinking again. About Kay. What else? Thinking that what happened to Kay…

'…wasn't my fault.' It just came out, all by itself.

'What, Sugar?'

'It wasn't my fault,' I said again. And then I told her. I really did – I told the blue sequinned DJ the whole story. Everything. How I had a best friend in high school. How we met, how we were always together. And I tried to stay as true to Kay's memory as I could. The words came like an erupting volcano that had been bubbling under the surface looking for a soft spot, a weakness. That poor woman, I bet she wished that she had never started smoking in the first place.

'So where is she then, this best friend of yours?' she asked.

'It wasn't my fault,' I said, again and the woman gave me a look that said stop talking shit. What's the story? Have you been drinking? All at the same time. So I told her the rest of it, not that she could have stopped me by that point anyway. This is what I was here for. Confession.

'I should have been there for her,' I said. 'She wanted to go to Santa Barbara for the weekend of Cinco de Mayo – you know Mexican Independence Day. They have this great celebration and we used to go up every year. We'd just finished college. But that weekend, I'd just met Bernie – that's my husband. I told Kay that I didn't want to go away with her. I wanted to see what happened with him. It was the first time I ever said 'no' to her and it took me two days to find the words to tell her. When I finally did, she didn't have much of a reaction, but said she was going without me. Didn't want to spend the weekend with me and my 'boyfriend,' she said. The next thing that happens – she's up there, she gets drunk on

Saturday night, steps into the road and is killed by a Greyhound Bus. It was the only Saturday night for seven years that I wasn't with her.'

The blue-sequinned DJ stared at me and lit another cigarette. I had her full attention. 'No kidding?' she said, 'your friend is dead?'

I was shaking now. Clenching my stomach and holding my back straight and as still as I could to stop myself shivering from head to toe. My teeth were even rattling, but I kept talking. Nothing could stop me.

'Bernie and I had the greatest weekend. We went to a movie – I can't ever remember what it was, but it was great. We had the best time, but still, all the while I had this bad feeling about letting her down. I couldn't shake it. I meant to say goodnight to him and drive up to Santa Barbara in the morning. I was worried about not being with her, I guess. But one thing led to another and Bernie and I...well you know and besides that we talked all night long. About everything. My throat was hoarse the next morning when the telephone rang, so Bernie answered it. He had to tell me. I thought, why would this nice guy tell me something like that. Had to drive me up to Santa Barbara. Didn't believe it – all the way I was saying there's been a mistake, it's not Kay. He was with me in the morgue when I identified her. Then we had to drive back to Northridge to tell her folks. He did the telling. I still didn't believe it, though I'd seen her. It was like a bad dream; I didn't believe it for years. I can't really believe it now as I'm telling you. In fact, I can't believe I'm telling you at all.'

I laughed a little, nervously. I tried to breathe

slower. A part of me wondered what her reaction would be, another bigger part of me didn't care, but the biggest part of me was thinking nothing. I was empty.

And then there was a tap on the door and a voice, a man's voice shouted, You're on and the singing outside stopped and the blue-sequinned DJ lifted herself from the chair, looked at me and started to leave. Before she left the room, she stubbed out what was left of her cigarette and said, 'Sugar, it wasn't your fault.'

After a minute, I followed her back into the ballroom. It looked as if the class of '87 were all in attendance now. So many people there. I looked around for one familiar face and found it – Bernie.

There he was cool as anything, like he belonged, crossing the room, carrying a bottle of champagne, two glasses. Smiling at everyone and looking for me.

He saw me just as the blue-sequinned DJ got onto the stage and started to speak. Welcoming the alumni of Hamilton High to the Sheraton Universal Hotel, introducing the reunion committee.

'Give them a round of applause for all their hard work in organizing this fabulous evening and tracking down nearly 600 people, 78 of which have come from out of state to be here tonight and one person, Melvin Marigold, along with his beautiful wife Maureen, has come here from their home in Paris, France to share this memorable occasion. How about another round of applause for them. And now class of 1987 find yourselves a seat because dinner is about to be served.'

This was followed by more applause and a massive movement of people.

Then Bernie was at my elbow, steering me to a table. Whispering in my ear that Harry had called, couldn't come, had second thoughts, couldn't walk in with Roger and couldn't walk in without Roger. Bernie thought he should come over in case I was all by myself.

He poured champagne into our glasses and introduced everyone to each other as our table began to fill up. There were two other couples and three women who wanted to sit together. I didn't know any of them; no cheerleaders or football players. Bernie went to find an extra chair for the extra lady and I began a conversation with the man sitting next to me. We were comparing our time in high school, of course. Had we known each other? He'd sung in the senior production of *Guys and Dolls*. Had to learn to dance for his part. Been voted Best Hands. Laughed, good-naturedly when I told him what the class had voted me. He introduced his wife. They lived in Texas now. He was in software. Had four children: three boys and one little baby girl, his wife leaned across him to say. And then Bernie was there between us, with his chair, already telling a joke. Talking so easily, the way he did everything.

As the meal came – the carrot soup, then the stuffed chicken, Bernie entertained everyone at the table with anecdotes about his dangerous job. He told the one about the time he took a group of South Korean businessmen abseiling in Malibu Canyon and had to convince one of them that it was better not to use his cell phone on the way down. I'd heard it before of course, but I had to admire the way he entranced new people so easily, so effortlessly, so like – Kay, actually. He dominated the proceedings. He brought the group together, found out about everyone, told more jokes, laughed heartily at everyone else's stories. The women at the table all smiled at me with every one of his punch lines, envious, interested in us. What a couple, aren't they great together, they were thinking. Edith Faz...something or other? Why don't we remember her from school?

After the coffee, Bernie whispered to me, do you want to dance or should we leave? I'll take you home. We can be alone. Would you like that? I've missed you. It would be good to be alone.

Just like Kay.

Just before we left, one of the women at the table gave me her phone number. 'Phone me sometime, we'll have coffee,' she said.

Oh, sure.

At my car, I said, 'Thank you for coming.'

'I'll meet you at home, right,' Bernie said. 'Follow me, my car's just over there. I'll drive it over here and then you can follow...'

'Bernie, I'm going home alone.'

'But why?' he said, 'we danced, we talked. I thought you were really glad to see me.'

I reached out to him. Touched his arm.

'I was. I am. But – I'm going home alone.'

I think it was only the second important decision

I've made my whole life. I think it was the right one and I was almost sure he would be okay.

But he pulled away. Turned his back on me and walked away, towards his car. I started to shiver for the second time that night. I felt cold, though it was August in LA.

I heard his car start and I watched him drive through the parking lot and down the hill. I watched his lights for as long as I could, but when he got to the bottom, I confused his car with all the other traffic and couldn't tell which way he went. I think he might have turned onto Sunset.

'Be safe, Bernie,' I whispered.

Gun Control

Last night, the dream again. The same dream, night after night and sometimes dream after dream. When it wakes me, I am demented for a moment or two. And then the strangest thing happens – my groggy mind tries to imagine an end. The end.

I hold the gun first in one hand, then using my other to keep it steady – point and pull hard on the trigger with my index finger. And bang! presto! my problem is gone.

But, here's the thing – I can't see who I am aiming at. Is it him or her? Sometimes I think (and I am always horrified by this) it is their child or their dog that is my target.

And that's the dream.

Then fantasy. What happens next? What outcome is there to my murderous execution? I would not go off into a bright future and a glowing sunset with him. Not now. Not after. Nor would I give her the false satisfaction of earned widowhood. Although it would suit her so: marital status without the despised sex. Quite possibly that's what she has now anyway. I imagine he is effectively castrated, but I have no way of knowing since. No, it's just a dream. My head trying to get revenge for the way my body wants him still. Hold the gun and aim. An easy, smooth power. That's probably all. There are no answers to the rest.

I went to work this morning and Jan, who manages the LoCost, told me that one of the customers wants to sell his gun. He confided in her about his reasons. She has the patience and the ready ears; the grey hair of a confidante and they all tell her. His reasons, she says, like she knows things no one else does, are political. There is an election coming and the parties are about to submit to popular demand of tighter gun control. This guy needs to dump his pistol, because no one would ever give him a licence for anything with his record. She tells me this with wide eyes and a big I-know-everything-about-everyone grin. She tells me the secrets of others because she thinks I am secretive myself: quiet; deep and arty and that somehow telling me private things about others will encourage me to share my own private things with her. She doesn't get it. I'm not deep – mostly I am just not interested. I don't care. When Jan goes home to her settled marriage, her two or three kids, I go home to my drawings (always black and white) and the cats.

Jan laughs often and when things aren't funny – high and thin and too sure. She was laughing as she taped up the notice this guy has prepared for the board, 'Who does he think could possibly be interested in buying a gun around here?'

When she went back to the storeroom, I wrote the phone number on my palm.

At lunchtime, I walked. Thinking about the gun. How

to approach. Imagine the conversation: Hello, Mr Green. I read your ad. How much for the gun? Will you show me how to use it? Or: Hello, Mr Green. How much for the gun? Will you tell anyone if I use it?

The prosecution will argue that I was hoping to see Brian. Hoping that he'd drive by in his beat up Rover, and thinking that I was stranded, offer to pick me up and...what? I don't know. For one thing, there was no car. He was on foot. And I, so busy thinking, did not even see him coming until he was there. In the middle of the busy High Sreet. Smiling. He was smiling.

'Coffee,' Brian said, as if this was normal. As if we saw each other here every day. And it was a statement.

Thank you God – I am irritated. Still, to him coffee is a statement of intention: Let's go to bed. Let's go to your place and go to bed. But my irritation did not show or turned to something else, because I must have smiled or changed my expression, and he said, 'No, I really mean coffee.'

Was the same expression stuck on my face like fly paper when we slid into either side of a booth at The Castell? Was I cool and in control? No, Your Honour, I was hot and agitated. It has been six weeks. And since then, I have wondered every day. I have wanted you every day. I have regretted. And I need to know what happened after. Have you been miserable and wretched? Has your life been filled with the sound of your wife's hysteria? Do I sit with you at every meal, sleep between you in your bed? Should I tell him that

133

I fantasise about shooting one of them, or myself, or even their dog? My crime needs structure.

Brian tried to make eye contact and never stopped talking. Finally he got up again to get our drinks. If I'd been calm, I would have walked out, leaving him standing alone with a cappuccino in each hand. But I didn't. I hadn't recovered from the last time I left him standing.

He came back to the table, sat down and started speaking. Case notes really: a brain-damaged boy showing signs that he might regain some of his speech. A matter of therapy – new methods. He had been searching for something that would excite the child so much that the desire to express would change a few limited sounds into words. I could feel the excitement of the project, but couldn't enter. Surely he knew that. I sat feeling dull, someone with nothing to say for herself, unable to contribute, too stupid to know anything about anything. Picking my fingernails in my lap. Then I saw his hands fiddling with the cup and saucer. Tearing at an empty sugar packet.

He was nervous. Good. Let him be nervous and let him talk and concentrate instead on memorising his voice and eyes. Two months ago there seemed no reason to ask for a photo or take one myself, and in the interim one of the hardest things to bear was not really remembering. If you draw someone, you will never forget what they look like. I have sometimes called myself an artist and yet I never took the time to sketch his face. I saw now that this eyes were green, not easily hazel, more like the colour of never changing willow. Now and again they flashed in a way I remembered. I did not dare let myself look at his mouth, but his voice was clear and strong. Once he told me that he would've liked to be a preacher. He was articulate and interesting. Sometimes funny. We'd laughed and fought. Discussed politics and modern art and television. Our friendship began and ended with debate, but it was the way he listened to me, weighed my importance. That was how he'd seduced me.

He did not look at his watch or at the other customers in the pub as he talked on and on, filling up the space for my unasked questions.

Finally he paused and looked at me closely, 'Another?'

The time, I thought. What the hell. 'No thanks. You go ahead.'

He came back with a real drink. A short. Maybe Scotch.

But I was sober, Your Honour. Whose honour? I have none left.

He drank. I said, 'So?'

'Let's go,' he said. I always liked command, actually. And this time I was not irritated.

LoCost lost out. We did the usual thing. I walked to my flat. He followed me five minutes later. The flat is over Boots, the chemist. Very convenient. I have lived here a long time. Brian fits in as if he has lived here too. He throws the cat from the bed and turns down the duvet. He strips off. He seems chunkier that I remembered. His legs are short, his body long and hairless. Heads for the shower. He knows that will please me. Wash her off you first.

It doesn't take long. It never did. Why did I think? And after, he talks some more, finally some of the questions are answered. He went straight back to her. Of course. I knew that. Straight back. Then the blame.

'It was you who didn't want me, you told me to go. What did you expect?'

Suddenly tired of him, I turn away and remember again the detached frenzy of the day he told his wife.

The phone rang. It was a Thursday. I'd just walked in the door from work. It will be Brian. I expected his call.

Hello, I purred – yes, purred – into the phone. The other voice was shrill and loud. The first thing I did was to hold the receiver away from my ear. Then I realised who it was, what she was saying and listened. First it was hysteria, accusations.

Did I know there was a child? They had a daughter, what about her? Did I know there were others? Did I know that he said he believed in God?

Later he arrived with a suitcase. She phoned again and sitting in my chair curled into a ball with a cat, I could hear her from across the room as he held the phone away from his ear and made patient noises which probably made her worse.

'She's ruined my life,' she screamed. I could hear him telling her that he was going to stay with me. He told her that he did not love her without any apology. I had never seen him cruel.

Then he brought the phone to me. I couldn't think.
I felt sick to hear her pleading. But when I took the
phone, she was quieter.

'Hello – I'm sorry,' I said. It sounded hopeless.

Then, very calmly, she offered him to me.

'He's not worth it,' she said.

I put the phone down and told him to go. I sent him
away. I thought I could see the reflection of my
weakness in his eyes. Her voice has been with me
since: *he's not worth it.*

'I'm too old to live with my parents, you know,' he was
saying. His breath smelled – or something. It might
have been his body.

In a movie we would have made love endlessly. The
big reconciliation scene. But no.

Instead he took my hand, 'Have you had a tattoo?'
he was looking at the number I'd written on my palm.

'Whose number?' Can he be worried? He thinks
that I have already found a new man whose phone I
can ring.

I laughed. Not like me, like someone in control.

His confidence is pretty low already. It's all a show.
His wife says he smells, he's not good in bed. She's
right. It's probably his fault that she hates sex. He
should not have told me so many of their secrets.

I took my hand away from him and got up from the
bed. I should have found him something for his
breath. I usually have gum around the place. I made a
move to find something, but really I wasn't doing
anything. Waiting for him to go.

Naked, I looked through my bag. It seemed to

arouse him. He came up to me from behind. His hands on my waist, I continued to search for mints or gum inside the bag.

'I probably can't manage it again, not just yet,' he whispered.

'Here take this.'

And he took the gum from my fingers and popped it in his mouth without a question.

Much later. He has gone. Back to her again, as he always will. There is no point, I'd finally said. Don't phone. Or. I think he was relieved actually. I know that I am.

Waking later from cats swimming in the black and white bath and happy shoppers dressed as mad cows, I see Mr Green's phone number on my hand. In the shower, I scrub it until it disappears.

~

Acknowledgements

These stories were formed in part by my work at the University of South Wales, the former University of Glamorgan, where I was lucky enough to bump into some of the best writing tutors and colleagues the world has ever known. Thank you to Catherine Merriman, Sheenagh Pugh, Chris Meredith, Tony Curtis, Meic Stephens for all kinds of teaching and special thanks to Rob Middlehurst for reading and commenting and reading again, but more important than all that sound advice was Rob's encouragement, enthusiasm and belief.

Many thanks also to so many generous readers and writing friends who have helped shape these stories with their comments, among them: Mike Thomas, Tom Anderson, Emma Darwin, Shelagh Middlehurst, Rhian Edwards and Jackie McKay.

Thank you to Derec Jones and his team at Opening Chapter, for always being professional as well as nurturing. Small presses regularly perform small miracles. I'm not sure how Opening Chapter achieves what it does with so little support.

My love and gratitude to Rhiannon Skivington and Ceri Llewelyn. I think the children of writers suffer a unique torture and these two have bore it with grace. And to my husband, Rick Wilson - I am so lucky! Thank you for your generosity and your patience.

Gun Control was first published as The End in Mama's Baby, Papa's Maybe (Parthian. 1999).

Thanksgiving and Another Las Vegas Story were published in Cambrensis.

Tattoo and Gather Gold were published in Square Magazine

His Shoes was published in Secondary Characters and Other Stories (Opening Chapter, 2015)

CPSIA information can be obtained at www.ICGtesting.com
Printed in the USA
LVOW11s2001150116

470669LV00001B/9/P